GRANT SAID, "LET ME TELL YOU ABOUT THE time Katie found a water moccasin in one of the sheds—"

Nessa abruptly clapped one hand over his mouth. "I don't want details! And the last thing I need is another lecture."

They were standing very close. Too close. The day's dying light aureoled her hair, mesmerizing him. He couldn't seem to help himself. As her fingers moved away from his lips to caress the nape of his neck, he slid one arm around to the small of her back and the other into that enticing mop of red-brown curls.

"What *do* you need?" he murmured.

All his good intentions forgotten, he covered her mouth with his.

I need this, Nessa thought. *And more.*

For a few delicious moments, she gave herself over to enjoyment. Then she pulled free. "Why now?" she asked in a whisper. "And why you?"

WHAT ARE *LOVESWEPT* ROMANCES?

They are stories of true romance and touching emotion. We believe those two very important ingredients are constants in our highly sensual and very believable stories in the LOVE-SWEPT line. Our goal is to give you, the reader, stories of consistently high quality that may sometimes make you laugh, sometimes make you cry, but are always fresh and creative and contain many delightful surprises within their pages.

Most romance fans read an enormous number of books. Those they truly love, they keep. Others may be traded with friends and soon forgotten. We hope that each LOVESWEPT romance will be a treasure—a "keeper." We will always try to publish

LOVE STORIES YOU'LL NEVER FORGET
BY AUTHORS YOU'LL ALWAYS REMEMBER

The Editors

Loveswept® 895

TRIED AND TRUE

KATHY LYNN EMERSON

BANTAM BOOKS
NEW YORK · TORONTO · LONDON · SYDNEY · AUCKLAND

TRIED AND TRUE

A Bantam Book / July 1998

ISBN 0-553-44643-6

Published simultaneously in the United States and Canada

ONE

"Just look at her, Hank. She's all wrong." Grant Bradley glared at the woman on the television screen and tried to ignore the fact that her throaty voice had an unwelcome effect on his libido.

"I'm looking, all right." Hank Gilbert flashed a lecherous grin before returning his attention to the videotape they were watching in Grant's office at Sidwell College. "You know what I see? I see high profile, which is exactly what we need if this project is going to cover its own expenses. She's not exactly hard on the eyes, either."

Grant had to concede the last point. Vanessa Dare was a fine-looking woman, slender and graceful. A close-up appeared on the screen, making him readjust his first guess at her age. Tiny laugh lines around her eyes put her on the other side of thirty, but not by much. Her hair was a brown far removed from his own nondescript shade. Red highlights that might or might not be natural played to the camera. So did eyes of a bright, electric blue. He wondered, as he shoved slipping spectacles back up his nose, if she wore colored contact lenses to achieve that particular hue.

"We're going to take a break now." She managed to sound as if she was speaking only to him, and making promises when she added, "Be sure to stay tuned for today's special feature, 'Bran: Is It Hallucinogenic?' "

A particularly annoying toothpaste commercial came on the tape recorded two days earlier. Grant grabbed the remote and hit the STOP button, returning the small set to regular programming, a game show he could ignore more easily than Vanessa Dare. "I've seen enough."

"Don't you want to know the truth about bran?"

"I know about bran, Hank. A large bowl of bran flakes may induce mild euphoria because wheat contains LSD, produced naturally by ergot, a common fungal infestation of wheat and rye that sometimes—"

"Whoa! It's more fun listening to the lady explain it. Besides, isn't that a little outside your area of expertise?" He made a show of looking at the name on Grant's office door. "Yep, still says Grant Bradley, Chairman, History Department. Still, you've probably got all kinds of things in common with Vanessa Dare. She'll be perfect for West-brook Farm."

"Hank, I'm staking my professional reputation and that of Sidwell College on this project. Do you seriously want me to risk everything on a pretty face?"

"She's no dummy, Grant." Taking the remote, Hank turned off the television. "You just saw that."

But Grant wasn't buying it. He'd watched her interview the head of an environmental group concerned about endangered species in western New York State. She'd managed to exude just the right combination of interest and journalistic neutrality, but all that meant was that Ms. Dare probably was a consummate actress. He'd just as soon not let another woman with a talent for deception into his life.

"She does a morning talk show, Hank. She reads lines someone else writes for her. It's all showbiz, no guarantee she has a brain in her head. Besides, what we have planned involves rough living. Anyone who looks like that will probably throw a tantrum if she breaks a fingernail."

Hank met Grant's objections with one unanswerable argument. "As chair of Sidwell's board of trustees, I control the money, Professor. And I say you need her."

Struggling to control his exasperation, Grant asked, "Why her? Why not someone from public television? This is a serious research opportunity for historians, not a tourist attraction."

"It had better be a bit of both."

Grant grimaced at the change in Hank's tone. He sounded like the lawyer and businessman he was, not like someone who'd been friends with Grant since their undergraduate days.

Crossing to his office's one floor-to-ceiling window, Grant stared at the walkway below and tried to gather his thoughts. It was snowing again. Spring was going to be late this year, another snag in his plans.

His reflection stared back at him, dark eyes troubled behind the glasses, forehead furrowed, jaw clenched. He willed himself to relax. Losing his temper wouldn't help anything. But damn he hated to compromise! For the last five years, he'd poured all his energy into almost single-handedly restoring Westbrook Farm. The hard physical labor had helped him put his life in perspective, even as his research had built the foundation for what he hoped to achieve academically.

"When I conceived the idea of creating a living history center," he said quietly, "it was to provide a place where scholars could experience firsthand what life was like in the 1890s. I intended it for people who already have a real appreciation of the tried-and-true methods of—"

"We've been through this before." Hank paused, as if gearing up for a summation to a jury. "You don't have a turkey's chance at Thanksgiving of succeeding with the project unless you catch the public's attention. Stir up enough interest and you're golden. Vanessa Dare is the perfect person to help you do that."

What Hank was really saying, Grant mused, was that he would advise the board of trustees to withdraw crucial funding if Ms. Dare wasn't part of the package. An ugly suspicion surfaced in Grant's mind. Did Hank, who had been divorced for several years, have a personal interest in the woman?

Hank popped the videotape out of the player. "I have it on good authority that she'll jump at the chance to produce a documentary. We can get her to immortalize Westbrook Farm at bargain-basement rates."

Grant turned from the window. "Why?"

"What does it matter? Ms. Dare has the know-how we need." Hank put on his best lawyer smile, the one he wore in TV commercials that urged clients who thought they had grounds for a lawsuit to give him a call. "All it will take now is a sales pitch from you. Lay on the charm and she's yours. She's single too."

"That's not a selling point." But when Hank started to toss the videotape into his briefcase, Grant stopped him. "Leave the tape."

Looking smug, Hank handed it over along with Vanessa Dare's business card. The address beneath her name was that of a television station in Syracuse, but another phone number had been

penciled in on the back. The handwriting was not
Hank's, nor did it belong to Ms. Dare, since above
the ten digits were the words "Call her at home."

After Hank left, Grant put the tape back in the
VCR and watched the hour-long show twice before he froze the frame on a close-up of its host-
ess. Those impossibly blue eyes looked back at
him. Her gaze seemed to be direct and guileless,
but he was certain acting ability was a prerequisite
for any media "personality." It was unlikely she
was as unaffected in person as she appeared on the
small screen.

Abruptly, he hit the OFF button and reached
for the card Hank had given him. He didn't have
any choice if he wanted Westbrook Farm to become a reality. He needed funding. To get it, he
would put up with far worse than Vanessa Dare.
He could endure a week in her company, in spite
of her alluring appearance, her sultry, low-pitched
voice . . . and the fact that she attracted him, on
a purely physical level, more than any woman he'd
encountered in a long, long time.

Three Weeks Later

"Stop trying to talk me out of going to Westbrook Farm, Craig," Vanessa Dare told her assistant. "I've made up my mind."

"Bad timing, Nessa. You know that. There's
talk of a syndication deal for your show."

"I'm not interested." To Vanessa's mind, there

were too many talk shows out there as it was. Besides, the last time she'd tried to tailor her style to meet corporate expectations had been a disaster. Right or wrong, she'd learned to go her own way, trust her own judgment. She compromised only when it was absolutely necessary for survival.

"You just like being a big fish in a little pond," Craig complained. "You're afraid to test the waters."

"Nice figure of speech." She had to smile. He was so transparent. It wasn't her career he was worried about, but his own. That he might also be correct didn't bother her.

Craig Seton was a few years Nessa's junior, and probably one of the best-looking men she'd ever met. Tall. Golden-blond hair. Bedroom eyes. Chiseled features. Body to die for.

And he left her cold. That might have worried her if she hadn't been too busy for romance anyway. Later, she thought, after she'd made it over this next career hurdle, she'd turn her attention to her personal life, maybe even look for a man to share it with.

She pretended to review the schedule of segments to be run during her "vacation," but she was really thinking that it would probably be a good thing to get away from Craig for a bit. He was becoming too attached to her. Whether he was drawn to her "star," as it supposedly rose toward greater fame, or to her person, as he kept claiming, he needed to get a life. If he wanted the bright lights of New York or L.A., he could go without her.

With luck, she'd have plenty of free time at Westbrook Farm to contemplate her future, in particular what she'd do if she did turn down a syndication deal. She couldn't simply stay where she was forever. The station had already suffered a few budget cuts. Her show was successful, but there were cheaper ways to fill that hour. Other syndicated shows, for example. If she was going to carve out a new career behind the camera, this was definitely the time to start.

"What is this place you're going to, anyway?" Craig asked. He still sounded sulky. "I've never heard of it."

"It's a real find, apparently. A site in the foothills of the Catskill Mountains that's been frozen in time since just before the turn of the century. The last of the family to own it was an eccentric lady who lived there alone, changing nothing for almost eighty years. After she died in the late 1970s, the place sat empty and abandoned until a history professor from Sidwell College discovered it and decided to restore it. He's offered me the chance to make a documentary about the trial run they're holding preparatory to opening the place as a living history center."

"Sounds dead boring to me."

Nessa ignored him. She'd always included short local history segments on her show and had enjoyed doing them. And if "dead boring" translated into a break from the hustle and bustle, then she was all for it.

"Well, give me your phone number," Craig said. "I think you're making a mistake, but if the network calls, I'll stall them until you can get back to them."

"Sorry, Craig. No phone." And it would take several hours to drive to Westbrook Farm too. No one was going to intrude on her privacy there. Bliss!

Craig looked appalled. "Surely you're going to take your cell phone. Please, Nessa. What about emergencies?"

"Maybe." He really did look upset, she thought. And she supposed it might be necessary to call out. But she certainly wasn't going to leave the phone on to receive incoming calls. And her beeper was staying home. In a bottom drawer. Underneath a stack of heavy sweaters.

Two days later, following the detailed map she'd been sent, Nessa turned off a little-used two-lane secondary road onto a dirt track. After a few twists and turns, it dead-ended in a parking area that contained a van with the Sidwell College seal painted on its side.

Success! Nessa eased her station wagon in next to the van and turned off the engine. Complete silence descended. If not for the other vehicle, she

would have sworn there wasn't another soul
around for miles.

No sign of habitation was in sight. No power
lines ran overhead. The narrow, muddy dirt road
she'd been following, however, resumed on the far
side of the parking area, winding toward a tree-
covered hillside. Somewhere up there was Westbrook Farm. She'd been warned she'd have to
walk part of the way in.

Sliding out of the station wagon, she stood and
stretched to relieve the stiffness in her back and
neck muscles, then glanced at her watch. The trip
had taken longer than she'd expected. She'd made
good time on Route 81 and on Route 17, but once
she'd turned off at Liberty, the going had been
slow. She hadn't really minded, though. She'd
found the hilly terrain attractive and the long
stretches between houses a nice change from the
heavily populated area she was accustomed to.

When she opened the back of the station
wagon and surveyed all the equipment she'd
brought, she hesitated. Transporting it would take
more than one trek up that hill. Should she scout
the area first, unencumbered? Or perhaps she
should just wait a bit and see if anyone else
showed up.

She looked again at the vehicle next to hers. It
was possible the others had all arrived together.
Only seven people, including herself and the professor who'd contacted her, were scheduled to

participate in the trial run. Six could easily fit into that Sidwell College van.

It seemed logical to assume everyone but herself was in some way connected to the tiny but prestigious liberal arts college where Dr. Bradley taught. Carpooling made sense. Sidwell was situated in Strongtown, a small city halfway between the only slightly larger city of Kingston and the town of Monticello, county seat of Sullivan County. By her best guess, the trip from Strongtown to Westbrook Farm would have taken about an hour.

Sighing, she reached for the field camera she'd borrowed from the station. She was probably the last one to arrive. Not the best way to make an impression.

Nessa had just lifted the camera out of the back of the station wagon when she caught sight of movement in the trees. A lone figure emerged and ambled down the hill toward her. Dr. Bradley? She blinked and stared.

When he'd first called her to invite her to make the documentary, she'd thought he sounded rather stiff and pompous, in spite of a deep, sexy voice. She'd therefore assumed he was in his fifties or sixties. If the man now entering the parking area and striding toward her was Grant Bradley, she'd been off by a couple of decades. True, his brown hair contained a few streaks of gray, but they added an air of distinction, not age. She'd guess he was somewhere in his late thirties.

He was also remarkably easy to look at. The hair was neatly trimmed but not too short. His features were regular with a hint of ruggedness, and possibly stubbornness, revealed in a strong jaw. His skin was smooth shaven. Nessa had never cared for that five-o'clock-shadow look some men seemed to think was sexy. The rest of his body wasn't bad, either, but she had only a moment to examine it before he spoke.

"Welcome to Westbrook Farm," he said in a voice that was unmistakably Grant Bradley's.

"Thank you," she said. "Has everyone else already arrived?"

"You just missed two of them, my student assistant, Mary Ellen Eldrich, and Jason Faulkner, on loan from Sidwell's theater department. They've gone to pick up a few more supplies and should be back shortly. Hank Gilbert is due later this afternoon. Bea and Doug Roper aren't coming until tomorrow. They're bringing the livestock."

To her dismay, Nessa's pulse rate speeded up at the news that she was alone in a remote location with this man. She tried telling herself she had no cause for alarm. Or for excitement, either. But there was something about Grant Bradley that made her very aware of him, more aware than she could ever remember being of anyone.

He wasn't even standing that close to her, she thought in dismay. He'd stopped a good six feet away to study her with as much intensity as she was regarding him. She tried to focus on his face, hoping to dispel the effect his whole body seemed to be having on her.

Wire-rimmed glasses perched on a rather nice nose, and behind the spectacles his eyes were a deep brown. Nessa's heart gave an odd little kick as his gaze skimmed over her. Her skin prickled. Annoyed, she tried to repress the reaction. She wasn't looking for a man. She didn't have time for that sort of thing.

"Love the suspenders," she said, blurting out the first safe comment that popped into her mind.

"They're called braces," he corrected her.

Whatever, she thought. They were still striking, made of silk and embroidered with bright flowers in five or six different colors.

He was dressed for the part of an inhabitant of Westbrook Farm in the 1890s, and the clothes of the last century flattered his lanky but muscular build. The braces held up wool trousers that, while loose, still hinted at nicely shaped thighs and calves. His linen shirt was open at the collar on this unusually warm April afternoon, and he'd rolled up the long sleeves to reveal forearms that appeared to have been developed by real work rather than workouts. His skin had a healthy tan and a light dusting of dark, curling hair.

Nessa frowned. How did he manage to stay in such good shape when he spent all his time in the ivory towers of academic life? The possibility that he'd taken a hands-on approach to the renovations at Westbrook Farm intrigued her.

He was still staring back at her. When she met his eyes again, she saw his expression change, and for a moment it seemed to her that he must have guessed what she'd been thinking.

If so, he was not pleased by her interest. A stiff formality imbued his words as he held out one hand. "I neglected to introduce myself," he said. "I'm Grant Bradley, Ms. Dare."

"It's nice to finally meet you, Dr. Bradley." Their handshake was brief, a slight pressure as skin met skin, but as Nessa withdrew her hand she was uncomfortably aware that it was tingling.

Oh, great! she thought. More evidence of chemistry at work between them. This was not the time for physical attraction to rear its ugly head. She had important work to do this week. Work that would require all her concentration. She did not need complications.

Determined not only to repress her reactions, but to use every means at her disposal to hide them from the man who caused them, Nessa reached into the open back of the station wagon. "How far to the house?" she asked without looking at him again.

The information he'd sent her had indicated the farm buildings were at the center of two hundred acres, mostly wooded. That and the fact that the nearest town, Luzon, was five miles away, were what had preserved the farm from vandals all those years. The only way in was the dirt track he'd just walked down. It wound upward toward a low ridge and disappeared into the trees.

"We have to cover approximately a half mile on foot," he said. "Eventually, we'll have a nine-passenger surrey available to transport guests and their luggage, but we haven't yet acquired either the buggy or a horse."

Nessa sorted through the equipment she'd brought, making two piles. After she'd locked the station wagon, she hoisted the camera and its accessories herself, leaving him to carry the duffel bag that was the sum total of her personal luggage.

There was a thoughtful expression on Grant Bradley's face when he caught up with her. She saw him glance down at the practical shoes she wore with her casual slacks and lightweight sweater.

"What? You expected me to show up in high heels and a short-skirted power suit?"

"I didn't know what to expect, Ms. Dare."

Before Nessa could reply, he launched into a lecture, telling her about the farm and its former inhabitants and sketching out the sort of thing he thought she should capture on tape. This was the Professor Bradley she'd talked to on the phone, a sexy voice that somehow managed to sound pedantic and a trifle arrogant.

Ease up, she wanted to tell him, but she didn't. Instead she reminded herself that she'd do well to dislike him. The more his superior attitude annoyed her, the better. Maybe, if he was irritating enough, she'd be able to squash that troubling prickle of awareness his nearness provoked.

Tuning in to what he was saying, she realized his ideas concerning the content of the documentary did not agree with hers. As the professor expected, there would be some shots of housekeeping nineteenth-century style and doing chores, all underscored by commentary. But since the participants would be taking on the roles of real people from a hundred years back, Nessa hoped to incorporate some vignettes that would typify activities of the time. If that week's volunteers proved to be passable actors as well as history buffs, she could foresee several lively segments to balance each information dump.

They reached the farmhouse after ten minutes of uneven walking. The white clapboard structure stood with its outbuildings in a clearing. From a distance it looked as charming as a Currier & Ives print. Up close the vision of an idealized pastoral scene got bogged down.

Obviously, Westbrook Farm had been enjoying the same spring thaw she'd experienced at home over the last few days, only in Syracuse the snow had all but disappeared. In these rural foothills, the temperature still dropped below freezing every night. Clumps of dirty, partially melted snow dotted the landscape, especially in the shady spots beside the barn and henhouse. Pools of brown water stood in the sun.

Mud season was not the most propitious time of year to film a documentary. It was going to be a challenge to make puddles and quagmires appealing. Then again, she'd always relished a challenge.

Gesturing for Nessa to go first, Grant Bradley ushered her across a wide porch that wrapped around two sides of the house. In the entry hall she caught only a glimpse of an old-fashioned parlor on her right before he opened the door directly in front of her to reveal a flight of stairs leading upward. On the second floor, he showed her into a large corner room filled with heavy oak furniture but dominated by a huge bed with an ornately carved headboard.

Nessa deposited the heavy bags she'd been carrying on the floor and rolled her shoulders in relief. She wasn't about to admit it aloud, but it had been a long time since she'd had to double as a packhorse.

"You'll find all the clothing you need in here," her companion said, reaching past her to open the standing wardrobe. The smell of cedar wafted out. When she moved out of the professor's way, he extracted several boxes from the capacious shelves. "What you have on now will go in storage while you're here, together with any other twentieth-century items you've brought with you."

"I beg your pardon?"

"You did agree to take on one of the staff assignments for this trial run, Ms. Dare."

"Yes, but—" She stopped speaking as he lifted a white cotton petticoat out of one of the boxes.

Several more items of intimate apparel were inside. She'd expected a costume. She'd sent dress and shoe sizes to the professor's assistant weeks ago with that in mind. But she hadn't given the matter much thought, and never had she imagined that the illusion would be so completely maintained.

"In the 1890s," he told her, "ladies wore bloomers, corsets, and what they called corset-covers under their clothes." He indicated a garment that resembled a lacy camisole, then the corset itself. "And at night, you'll wear this."

The nightgown he unfolded and spread before her on the bed was intended to cover the wearer from neck to toes. It was beautiful, all but dripping with lace, but a far cry from the wash-softened college football jersey and kneesocks that were Nessa's usual choice.

Such nightwear called up images she was reluctant to contemplate. Romantic. Seductive. Her fingers itched to touch the fine fabric, but she fought the urge and glowered at Grant instead.

"You are not," she said firmly, "deciding what I wear to bed."

TWO

Grant met Vanessa's defiance with what he hoped was an enigmatic expression. One thing was clear to him now that he was looking very closely into her eyes. She did not wear contact lenses. The color around her widening pupils was definitely electric blue. A current seemed to arc from those snapping orbs, setting off sparks every time her gaze touched him.

He dropped his own gaze, only to wonder why he hadn't noticed her lips when he'd watched that videotape. They were hard to ignore. Slightly pouty, just begging to be kissed even when, as now, they were pursed in annoyance. The faint, clean scent of Ivory soap came to him as he took a step closer to her, startling him into stopping in his tracks. He'd expected to get a whiff of some expensive perfume.

An impulse to tease her also took him by sur-

prise, making him speak before he thought
through how his words might be taken. "Consider
yourself lucky we aren't recreating the sixteenth
century. They slept in the nude back then."

"Thank you so much for sharing that with
me." Gingerly, she picked up the nightgown and
held it in front of her. "Not my style," she concluded.

Grant watched her, perplexed by his own behavior. Making suggestive remarks to women he'd
just met was *not* like him. What was it about Vanessa Dare that had made him say something like
that? She hadn't been flirting with him. Just the
opposite.

In self-defense, he automatically slipped into
lecture mode. "As I explained to you on the
phone, in return for being given the opportunity
to make this documentary, you will assume the
role of Katie Westbrook for the duration of your
stay."

"Yes, I know. Katie was the only daughter still
at home in the 1890s." Vanessa gave him a look he
couldn't interpret. "You sent me reams of information about her life up to that time. And I understand that when the living history center is
open, someone on the permanent staff will assume
her role. I've seen something similar done at
Plimoth Plantation."

He nodded approvingly. The Plymouth, Mas-
sachusetts, of today existed side by side with a re-
creation of the Pilgrim settlement of the 1620s.

Staff members were assigned the identity of specific historical figures and immersed themselves in their characters, right down to learning and using each individual's native regional accent.

"Well, then, I'll leave you alone to get changed." He couldn't resist adding, "If you need any help getting into the corset, just give a holler."

Grant had never intended that she actually wear the corset and had provided one only so she could see what it looked like. He headed for the door without telling her so, however, driven by a whim to discover if she'd try to comply or simply ignore his instructions.

"Wait a minute," she called after him. "Where's the bathroom?"

He paused in his retreat long enough to open the front of the washstand with a flourish, revealing a china chamber pot. "We also have an outhouse."

"No bathroom?"

"I did warn you we'd be roughing it. No television or telephone. No electricity, hot and cold running water, or central heating, either."

They stared at each other in silence for a moment. Then she nodded, surprising him yet again by accepting all his pronouncements without fuss or complaint. "Where will I find you when I'm dressed?"

"Come out to the barn. We'll start there, and I'll give you the grand tour."

"Fine."

He hesitated a moment longer and felt one corner of his mouth kick up as he looked at her. "You'll do," he said.

"I'll do what?" Something of the saucy wench was in her voice. And the sultry woman of the world. It was a potent combination, one he ordinarily would have found appalling.

Grant hadn't let himself respond to any woman's wiles since that debacle six years back. He'd always thought that if he did get involved in a relationship again, it would be with a quiet little mouse of a woman, someone who would always defer to him and never make demands.

"I wouldn't touch that line for any amount of money," he said, but his half smile had turned into an appreciative grin.

Nessa was more likely to turn out to be a barracuda or a black widow spider than a mouse, but he couldn't deny that he was powerfully drawn to her. This next week was going to be . . . interesting.

Again he turned to go. Again she called after him. "If I'm Katie Westbrook," she asked, "who are you portraying?"

On his way out of the room, he casually tossed the answer over his shoulder. "Why, Katie, I'm Simon Hanlon, your sister Emmaline's widower." He paused for effect. "The man you're eventually going to marry."

Her small, startled gasp amused him. This time he didn't even try to restrain his reaction.

"That was *not* in the bio you sent," Nessa grumbled to herself as the sound of Grant Bradley's rich, deep laughter faded.

Left alone to change her clothes, she felt momentarily disoriented. She wasn't sure what to make of Professor Bradley, except that he'd done a number on the calm, collected facade she usually presented to the world.

When she'd agreed to make this documentary, he'd sent her a forty-page computer printout filled with background material on the project and on her assigned role. Nowhere had there been mention of a boyfriend or lover or future husband for Katie. There *had* been something about the year being 1890, though. If Nessa remembered rightly from her long-ago visit to Plimoth Plantation, the "residents" there refused to admit to any knowledge of events that happened after the year they were re-creating. Apparently they would be doing something similar here. Perhaps the romance between Simon and Katie had yet to begin.

As Nessa stripped off her sweater and slacks and reached for the chemise Grant had left on the bed, that conclusion didn't make her feel less uneasy about her intense reaction to the handsome professor. Goose bumps erupting all up and down her arms and legs, however, focused her attention on a more immediate concern. She hadn't realized until that moment just how chilly it was in the room.

No central heating. No fireplace, either. At least not in her bedroom. Maybe she would be wearing that nightgown after all . . . over her nightshirt and socks and the L.L. Bean ladies' long johns she'd packed in her duffel bag.

Shivering, she slipped into the chemise, corset cover, bloomers, and several petticoats, even the one that supported the bustle, putting them on top of her modern underwear. She ignored the corset, as she was quite sure Dr. Bradley expected her to. For one thing, there was no way she could get into it without someone's assistance, even if she had been inclined to try.

The dress she found hanging in the wardrobe wasn't difficult to manage alone, in spite of dozens of tiny buttons. Fortunately, they were all in the front. The dark blue garment was beautifully made. Cashmere, she thought, trimmed in silk. The little bustle at the back gave it a jaunty look. Three-quarter-length sleeves were decorated with silk braid and white lace at the cuffs, and the skirt, which just cleared the ground, had two rows of matching braid around the bottom. She found two pairs of shoes, dainty slippers made of black leather and sturdy ankle-high boots. Remembering the state of the track they'd followed from the parking lot to the house, she donned the latter.

All that was left was to pin on the small cameo

designed to hold the collar of the dress together. She stood in front of the mirror attached to the dresser to do that, inhaling the pleasant scents of furniture polish and lavender sachet. Once she'd made sure the brooch was straight, she surveyed the rest of her appearance.

Her hair was all wrong. She found hairpins in a ceramic dish and tried to style her shoulder-length curls, but it was hopeless. There was no way to force them into any style appropriate to the nineteenth century.

A small piece of white fabric still lay on the bed. When Nessa picked it up, she realized it was a cap with a frilled edge and a puffed crown. She made a face, but plunked the frothy confection on top of her head and once more studied her image in the mirror.

Turning this way and that after she anchored the cap with pins, she decided that, all in all, her reflection pleased her. She looked reasonably authentic, and the dark blue bodice shaped her breasts as if it had been tailored to her precise measurements. Nessa frowned at that thought. The perfection of the fit was quite remarkable, considering all she'd given out was that she normally wore a size ten. Someone, she concluded, had a good eye, or had spent quite a bit of time watching her on the video she knew had been sent to Hank Gilbert. She supposed she should feel flattered. And she would, she decided, if everything about Grant Bradley didn't already rattle her. What on earth had possessed her to throw out a double entendre that way? Especially after her vow not to let him know how he affected her.

"You'll do," she repeated aloud, mimicking Grant. "I'll do what?" she added in her own voice. "You'll do nothing," she told her image in the mirror. Except turn out a damned good documentary.

A few minutes later, Nessa left the house. Before she began to make her way along the muddy path to the barn, she paused to close her eyes and inhale deeply. The air smelled like spring, and right in the sun it felt almost like summer.

Tomorrow, she thought, looking up at the clear blue sky, it might snow. Or rain hard enough to cause flooding. Or the thermometer might shoot up to eighty degrees. Ordinarily, she liked unpredictability, but in this situation she didn't want to have to jump any extra hurdles. Not in an ankle-length dress, anyway.

It felt surprisingly comfortable, she realized as she walked toward the barn. The fabric was both wonderfully soft and toasty warm. But there were problems with this whole business of wearing a costume, issues that needed to be addressed without further delay. Squaring her shoulders, she walked up a ramp and through the huge open door to the barn.

Because it had been so cold in the house, Nessa expected the chill that greeted her within, but after the brightness outside, she also needed a moment for her eyes to adjust to the shadows. Despite the door being open and dusty sunbeams filtering in through several windows, the daylight did little to dispel the darkness of the barn's cavernous interior.

She advanced a few cautious steps, aware of the scents of sawdust and hay. Somewhere ahead of her she could hear a rhythmic thunking sound. She moved toward it, past a row of grain bins and a workroom.

When she found the source of the noise, Nessa swallowed, her throat suddenly dry. She'd been right earlier. Grant Bradley did not spend all his time in a classroom.

A splitting maul gripped in both hands and raised above his head, he stood bare-chested before a chopping block, taking aim at a section of tree trunk that must have been a good foot in diameter. As Nessa watched, the blade came down with force enough to cleave the wood in two. Barely pausing, he repositioned one of the halves and struck it again, once more rending it in two. With each descending blow, the muscles in his arms and torso rippled.

Unable to help herself, Nessa stared at him until he apparently sensed he was no longer alone and looked up. Lord, the man had a sexy smile! She felt as warm as if she'd been the one chopping firewood. Helpless to do otherwise, she watched him pick up a towel to wipe his face and chest, then don his shirt once more.

Now there was a scene for a movie, she thought. But not for the one she was making. If she put what she'd just seen into her documentary, she'd have to start considering the line between a PG and an R rating.

"Hello, Katie," he said.

"Simon." She cleared her throat. "You said you'd give me a tour."

"I always keep my promises." He indicated the area all around them. "This level is called the threshing floor."

With that, he launched into detailed descriptions of every nook and cranny of the barn, leading her from place to place to point out the highlights. It was a relief to hear him lecturing again. Nothing sexy about a stuffy professor droning on and on. Or so Nessa tried to tell herself.

As she trailed after him, she concentrated on listening to what he was saying, but also considered what scenes she could shoot in the barn. His nearness and the resonance of his voice kept distracting her. Preoccupied, she failed to watch her footing and ended up stumbling on a section of uneven flooring.

One of Grant's big hands shot out to steady her, slipping around her waist. At his touch, her stomach flip-flopped. She looked up, then couldn't stop staring. His broad shoulders and lean, athletic torso were silhouetted by the window at his back. That sight, combined with the proximity of their bodies and the feel of his strong arm encircling her, acted like an electric current, tingling deliciously and at the same time shocking her with its intensity. In sudden panic, she tried to pull free. He reacted by tightening his hold.

"What's wrong?" he asked.

"Nothing. Sorry. You just caught me by surprise."

His gaze swept over her, as if to assure himself she really was all right. "That outfit looks good on you," he said, "but you've got the cap on backwards."

With deft fingers, he unpinned her headgear, turned it around, and settled it properly in its place. "There. Much better."

His hand brushed her cheek, and she jerked her head back, her startled gaze colliding with his. For a long moment, neither of them spoke.

Slowly, a knowing smile transformed his features from stern into sexy, triggering an immediate reaction in Nessa. Her mind formed pictures of the bedroom she'd been assigned, and the antique bed she'd already noticed was way too big for one person. Well, *there* was an obvious solution to the problem of sleeping in an unheated room every night.

She blinked hard, struggling to regain her composure. Why was she having so much difficulty remembering why she'd come out there? She'd had a legitimate reason for ending up alone in a dimly lit barn with a man who was having a most peculiar effect on her heart rate. Unfortunately, at the moment, that reason eluded her.

"You aren't wearing the corset," he said as his hands settled at her waist. "If you were, and it was properly laced, my fingers would meet."

Grant knew he ought to release her, but he couldn't. Not just yet. In the first instant of contact, he'd felt the jolt right down to his toes. Touching her now made him feel alive in a way he'd never known before. His hands slid upward until his thumbs rested just beneath her breasts. Vanessa stared back at him, her eyes wide, her expression bemused, as if she were equally confused.

His fingers drifted down, then back up to curve behind her rib cage and draw her closer.

"No," she said, sounding breathless and not at all convincing.

Reluctantly, he released her anyway.

The physical link was broken, but eye contact held. He recognized in her expression bewilderment warring with arousal, an echo of his own reaction. He expected irritation to come next, since he sensed she didn't want to be attracted to him any more than he wanted to want her.

He had to give her credit for aplomb. She drew herself up straighter and spoke in a haughty voice, apparently having decided to pretend the moment they'd just shared had never happened. "You didn't expect me to wear that corset," she informed him. "This dress was made to fit my natural waist."

"Give the lady a gold star," he shot back. Ignoring the chemistry between them was a damned fine idea. "Not even for the sake of historical accuracy would I put someone's health and well-being at risk."

"Compromise, Professor?"

"Only when absolutely necessary." He wasn't an unreasonable man.

"I'm glad to hear it's at least possible, because we need to discuss another aspect of this costume business."

"Clothing," he corrected automatically.

"Excuse me?"

He watched her fuss with a lock of her hair, apparently without realizing she was doing it, winding it first one way and then the other around her finger. She wasn't quite as calm as she pretended to be. The observation cheered him considerably.

"We're not performing in a play, Ms. Dare. This is a reenactment. We wear clothing, not costumes."

"Whatever. I do appreciate that you want everything to be as authentic as possible, but—"

"You won't get it into a bun that way."

It took her a moment to understand his remark. Then, embarrassed, she tucked the strand of hair she'd all but twisted into a corkscrew back up under the cap he'd adjusted.

"If you want, I can get you a wig. Set in a chignon, perhaps."

"I'm not worried about my hairstyle."

"Oh?" His gaze returned to the mangled curl.

"No. It's the dress that's the problem. I cannot work in a floor-length garment. You invited me to join you here so that I could make a documentary about the project. To do that, I need to be able to move freely."

"Many women managed quite well in outfits just like the one you're wearing."

"I doubt that Katie Westbrook wore a bustle while she scrubbed the floor."

"There's another dress in the wardrobe without one. If you'd taken the time to examine—"

"It's still floor-length. For the kind of work I'm here to do, I need to wear pants." She glanced around the barn. They'd left the threshing floor and were now in the area where animals would be kept. "Take that stall, for example. In order to get the best angle for a shot of someone milking a cow, I'd want to be up there." She pointed to a square opening into the hayloft above. "And for some exterior scenes, I'll need to climb halfway up a tree for the perfect shot. If you think I can manage in a long skirt and a half-dozen petticoats, then I invite you to put on a similar outfit and give it a try."

She had a point, but Grant wasn't ready to concede it. "Why can't you simply set up the camera and pan the action?"

"What did you do? Read one book on camcorders? Have you had any experience shooting either film or video?"

"What experience do you need? Eight-year-old kids make home movies these days."

"Only the obvious fact that you believe that to be true is preventing me from losing my temper," she warned him. She didn't bother, however, to keep the sarcasm out of her voice. "If you'd like to bring in an eight-year-old, feel free, but if you want a professional job done on your precious project, Professor, then you'd best let me decide what will work and what won't. If you place restrictions on me, the results will reflect that."

Grant leaned against the manger pole. "Explain what your work involves," he said.

She stood, hands on hips, glowering at him for a full minute before she took him up on his invitation. "Let me give you the short course then, Professor. Making a documentary involves more than just pointing a camera. Shots have to be planned in advance. I need to consider framing my subjects and the lighting and how close I want to be, as well as what's happening in the scene. In addition, when I'm ready to shoot, I have to be aware of sounds. An omnidirectional microphone will pick up everything from a barn swallow nesting in the rafters to your own grumbling because you tripped on that loose board that nearly sent me flying earlier. In some situations I will use the unidirectional mike, which only picks up audio directly in front of itself. In order to make smooth transitions, visually and audibly, I will need to move unhampered by long skirts."

"I'd have thought you could edit the tape afterward to fix anything that wasn't right."

"I was given to understand that you, and I, have severe time and budget restrictions, Professor." Her smug smile told him she realized that blow had hit home.

"What do you have in mind for interior shots?" he asked, changing the subject slightly.

He trailed after her as she sketched out several scenes that could be taped in the barn. She was all set to take him outside and lecture him on the use of available light when he pulled a gold watch out of its pocket, popped open the cover, and frowned at the time.

"Jason and Mary Ellen should be back shortly. We'd better get a move on if you want a quick tour of the house before they get here."

"There's no sense in going anywhere unless we reach an agreement on this issue of clothing."

"You agreed to participate in our trial run." He didn't give her time for a comeback. "If you will produce, direct, and act in the documentary, you can keep your own clothes for use as necessary. What do you think?"

"I think it was pretty high-handed of you to decide my possessions should be confiscated in the first place. Just as a matter of curiosity, how do you plan to deal with nonclothing items belonging to the re-enactors who will pay for the privilege of coming here? Are they to be forced to exchange Ivory for lye soap? Do without shampoo? Abandon deodorant and mouthwash? Even the most avid history buff is going to be reluctant to give up every advantage of twentieth-century life."

"Ivory soap was first sold in 1879. Listerine was introduced in 1880."

"Thank goodness for small favors."

"Do we have a deal, Vanessa?"

"Nessa," she corrected him.

"Actually, I'll be calling you Katie while you're here."

"Not when I'm working."

He felt as if they were hammering out the clauses in a legal contract. "Agreed, if you will attempt to stay in the character of Katie Westbrook when you aren't working."

"That depends."

"On what?" The woman was beginning to exasperate him. He didn't think he was asking all that much of her.

"What that means in relation to you."

"To me?"

"You said Katie eventually married Simon. Is she smitten with him now? How does he feel about her?"

"Ah." Good question, even if it did make him uncomfortable. "Katie's mother, Ella Westbrook, adamantly opposed the idea of any man marrying his late wife's sister. So, although Simon lived here after his wife, Emmaline, died, he and Katie were obliged to be circumspect. Less than a month after Ella's death, however, they eloped and left Westbrook Farm forever."

"A real love story then?"

He shrugged. "Maybe we'll find out more while you're here."

About Katie and Simon, he thought, and perhaps about themselves too. Disturbed by the wayward direction of his thoughts, Grant was relieved to hear voices outside the barn. Jason and Mary Ellen had returned, preventing Nessa from asking further questions.

THREE

Nessa lingered in the barn after Grant left to greet his returning volunteers. She wondered where Katie might have met for tête-à-têtes with her future husband. Here in the barn? She supposed that was one likely possibility. Her gaze went to the hayloft above. She had no trouble at all imagining a secret rendezvous, Grant Bradley portraying Simon, and in Katie's role—

"Cut it out," she told herself in an annoyed whisper. Such flights of fancy were dangerous. Grant Bradley was not some romantic hero out of the last century, no matter how good he looked in the clothes. He was a stuffy, egotistical, inflexible college professor, and she'd do well to remember that. Besides, she was at Westbrook Farm for a purpose. She had a job to do, a future to build. She did not have time for distractions.

Three people waited for her outside the barn.

On their way into the house, this time via a small back stoop, Grant introduced Dr. Jason Faulkner, head of the Sidwell College theater department. A few years older than Grant and about fifty pounds heavier, Faulkner had a "smoker's face."

Nessa had done a segment for her show on that topic and caught herself staring at Faulkner. He exhibited the classic facial features, especially crow's-feet at the corners of his eyes, wrinkles radiating at right angles from his lips, and deep lines on the lower jaw. Combined with a leathery look to the skin and a slightly gray complexion, those clues suggested that he was, or at one time had been, a heavy smoker.

"And this is Mary Ellen," Grant was saying as they went inside. "She's Molly, the hired girl, otherwise known as the maid of all work. She'll be cooking, doing laundry, beating rugs—all the normal 'woman's work' around a farm."

Startled, Nessa looked harder at the petite young woman at Grant's side. In her early twenties and dressed in snug blue jeans and a bosom-hugging turtleneck, she had ash-blond hair, wide blue-green eyes, and a perky smile. She also gave the impression that a good wind could blow her away.

"Don't worry, Ms. Dare," Mary Ellen assured her. "I'm stronger than I look." As if to prove it, she set about starting a fire in the nickel-plated woodstove. Although she spoke to Nessa, explaining what she was doing and why, her gaze returned repeatedly to Grant, as if she silently sought his approval.

"You're definitely more than you seem," Jason remarked. His smirk told Nessa he'd noticed something odd about the young woman's behavior too.

"Mary Ellen is a world-class gymnast, among other things," Grant said.

Among other things, Nessa decided, Mary Ellen had a world-class crush on her professor. A nervous quality in her voice combined with the adoration in her eyes gave her away. It was not just hero worship, either. Nessa was reminded of the scene in *Raiders of the Lost Ark* when one of "Dr. Jones's" students sat in his class, blinking at him, the words "I Love You" written on her eyelids. Nessa wondered if Grant realized just how deep his assistant's devotion went.

Jason had dropped the grocery bags he'd carried in onto the scrubbed pine table and now wandered over to peer out a window. "There's Hank," he said, "but who's that with him?"

Grant retraced his steps to the back door. "He's a stranger to me."

Nessa went to stand beside him. Just one surprise after another, she thought as she recognized the tall blond man striding toward the house. "I know him," she said aloud.

"Hank Gilbert?" Grant sounded suspicious.

She glanced at the older of the two approaching figures. She had never met her friend Taffy's significant other, but she recognized Hank from a photo she'd seen. In person he looked just as slick and self-centered. Typical lawyer. She'd distrusted the breed since childhood, but they had their uses.

"No," she told Grant. "I know the other man. Craig Seton." A sinking feeling in the pit of her stomach, she waited for the two men to enter the kitchen. Maybe Craig had just stopped by on his way to somewhere else.

Fat chance.

Hank Gilbert came in first, his smarmy smile in place. "Brought a new recruit," he announced, and Nessa had to swallow back a groan.

Craig stepped inside, a patently phony look of pleasure on his boyishly handsome face. It slipped when he got his first good look at what she was wearing. His eyes widened as he took in Grant's garments. That Mary Ellen and Jason still wore modern clothing completely baffled him, but being Craig he wouldn't admit to being confused.

"Hey, nice duds," he said, trying to sound enthusiastic. Before anyone could respond, he engulfed Nessa in a much-too-intimate hug, then kept his arm around her shoulders to pull her aside for a private moment. "What's with the costumes?" he whispered.

"They aren't costumes," she hissed back. She had to force herself not to squirm in his embrace. "I didn't expect to see you here, Craig."

"Couldn't let you brave the wilds all by yourself. I talked Mr. Gilbert into inviting me to participate."

"Oh?" She arched an eyebrow. "And who are you going to be?"

"Pardon?" Craig asked. It was obvious he hadn't a clue how things worked at Westbrook Farm.

She shrugged free of his arm. "Each of us has an assigned role," she told him. "That of a person who was at Westbrook Farm in 1890." She no longer bothered trying to keep her voice low. She suspected every word they'd already said had been clearly audible. The kitchen wasn't all that big.

As if to prove her right, Grant took up the explanation, telling Craig that permanent staff, some paid, some students earning graduate credit, would assume the identities of the farm's residents when the living history center opened. "Bea and Doug Roper, who arrive tomorrow, are on board for the first six months. They'll be Ella and Tunis Westbrook. This week, to test both the program and the physical surroundings themselves, volunteers are taking the other staff roles. The Westbrooks had three grown children still at home. Katie, that's Nessa. Nathan"—he indicated Jason, who gave a mock bow — "and Josiah."

While Craig looked dazed, Grant went on to introduce Mary Ellen and explain her role, and told Craig that he, Grant, was "the widowed son-in-law and father of the Westbrooks' only grandchild."

That caught Nessa by surprise. "Simon was a father?"

Grant glanced her way. "Of course. Tess's father."

A Tess had been mentioned in the information he'd sent, Nessa remembered, but she was sure it had said only that she was Tunis and Ella's granddaughter, not that she was Simon's child.

Grant continued. "Tess was the one who lived here at the farm until she was an old woman, never changing much of anything, not even adding power or plumbing. She was born Tess Hanlon, but she always went by the name Tess Westbrook."

"Why?" Craig asked. He still seemed confused. Nessa couldn't blame him.

"That's unclear. She was seventeen when Katie and Simon eloped in 1897. Apparently she rarely left the farm after that. Never married. Eventually, she was the only one of the family left."

Nessa was only half listening to Grant's answer. A disturbing image had crept into her mind—Grant with a dark-haired, dark-eyed daughter. She suddenly realized that although she knew Simon's marital status, she had no idea what Grant's was. Did he have a wife? Children?

Obviously unaware of her thoughts, Grant went on to tell Craig that some of the re-enactors who would be there that week had had a hand in planning and implementing the project. "Jason is here, for example, because the costume shop in his theater department provided the clothing. Hank is our legal eagle. Because he needs to go back to Strongtown at least once over the next few days, he's taking on the part of a boarder. During 'live-ins,' teachers seeking recertification, undergraduate students, and history buffs will take on those roles."

"The paying customers," Hank clarified. "I thought Craig could handle the part of another guest. Or maybe play Katie's younger brother."

"You're Katie?" Craig asked Nessa, finally catching on.

"Yes." Her gaze drifted to Grant, who had been willing enough to lecture Craig but still did not look pleased about having a newcomer thrust upon him.

"I don't want to be your brother," Craig declared. "Guess that leaves a guest, like Mr. Gilbert suggested."

"No, I have a better idea," Grant said.

Nessa glimpsed the dangerous gleam behind his glasses and had a sudden premonition that her "vacation" at Westbrook Farm was not going to provide the calm and peaceful respite she'd been hoping for.

"We need someone to take on the persona of Jake Lounsbury," Grant said. "Why, now that I think about it, I can't imagine how we'd manage without him."

Puffed up with self-importance, Craig fell

right into the trap. "Well, sure. I'll do what I can. Who is he?"

Grant smiled, the same kind of smile that had been on his face when he'd told her that Simon Hanlon had married Katie Westbrook. "Why, he's the hired man," he told Craig. "The one who'll be milking the cows and mucking out the horse's stall and slopping the hogs for the next week."

"He was joking, right?" Craig asked Nessa. "About me taking care of all those animals?"

Roughly thirty minutes after his arrival at Westbrook Farm, Craig appeared in the doorway of the sitting room, where he'd arranged to meet Nessa. He was wearing the extra set of clothes Grant had brought for himself, having changed into them in the room in the barn the two men were sharing.

Nessa fought a smile. Her assistant looked miserably uncomfortable. She really should not find his situation funny, but it was difficult to hold back her mirth.

"You do look the part," she managed to say before a sputter of laughter escaped her.

In construction his garments were almost identical to Grant's, though the braces were plain and the pants were blue denim, but on Craig the shirt bagged at his shoulders and chest, while the trousers were noticeably snug at the crotch and a couple of inches too short. Craig's Italian leather shoes didn't quite go with the rest of the outfit. Grant, she recalled, had been wearing some kind of work boots.

"All I need is a piece of grass to chew on and I'll look just like a hayseed," Craig grumbled. Smiling sheepishly, he added the ultimate touch by donning the most god-awful straw hat Nessa had ever seen.

The sight was too much for her. Laughter rippled out of her until her eyes filled with tears.

"Jeez, get a grip, will you, Nessa," Craig said. "This was your idea," he added, ignoring the fact that she had not invited him to come after her.

"I'm sorry." She choked and sputtered. "Really. I am." She had to turn away from him to get control of herself.

For a moment she stared at the portraits hanging on the wall in front of her without really seeing them. Then her eyes suddenly focused and she grimaced, all desire to laugh gone. She had no doubt in her mind who those two picklepusses were—Ella and Tunis Westbrook, Katie's overbearing parents. The ones who'd kept her from marrying the man she loved until after Ella's death.

Ella was distinguished by a hawk nose upon which perched little round glasses much like the ones Grant was wearing. Beneath that were a sharply pointed chin and a formidable bosom. Tunis struck Nessa as equally unappealing. His slightly bovine features looked out at her with the stiffness of a self-important Dutch burgher of an earlier time.

"I've never seen so many pictures," Craig said.

Scanning the other walls, she saw that there were indeed an abundance of them, a hodgepodge of artwork covering every available inch of wall space. Prints. Charcoal sketches. Watercolor landscapes.

"Good thing," Nessa said. "If they weren't there, we'd have to live with the nauseating pink cabbage roses on the wallpaper."

Craig caught her hand and tugged her toward the sofa, a heavily carved piece of furniture with roll-over arms. "We need to talk while the rest of them are still upstairs," he said.

"Yes, we do." She sat carefully, arranging bustle and skirts. She'd thought about changing into jeans, but since she didn't intend to start shooting until the next day, she'd decided to humor the professor.

"Jeez. What's this thing covered in?" A moment after he'd plunked himself down next to her, Craig was up again, glowering at the upholstery.

"Horsehair, I think." She glanced at the other chairs. All were equally massive, equally carved. Black walnut, probably. Only the settee was covered in softer red plush.

Gingerly, Craig eased himself back onto the sofa, but she could tell by his fidgeting that he wasn't comfortable. Horsehair was prickly stuff, and he had only two layers of fabric between it and his skin. It appeared there were advantages to multiple petticoats after all.

"We need to talk," he said again.

She nodded. She wasn't looking forward to this little chat, but she supposed they might as well get it over with. "Why did you follow me here, Craig?"

"Hey, Nessa. You know how I feel about you. I couldn't stand the thought of our being separated for a whole week."

"Give me a break, Craig."

"It's at least part of the reason I came."

She almost believed him. He did sincerity well. "What's the other part?"

"You would have been out of touch otherwise."

Translation: He'd brought his pager and cell phone. And probably his notebook computer too. Nessa sighed. "That was the idea. I needed to get away."

"From me?" He looked hurt.

"From everyone. Everything." She toyed with the fringe on a large pillow propped up on the arm of the sofa. Silk-screened onto the fabric was a picture of "the eighth wonder of the world"— the Brooklyn Bridge.

"Including heat?" Craig asked. "Bathrooms? Nessa, this is insane!"

"Well, it appears you've agreed to go insane

right along with me. You didn't need to say you'd stay, Craig."

"Yes I did," he said stubbornly. "Someone has to look out for your interests."

"I can look after my own interests, thank you very much. And myself too." With an effort, she controlled her temper. She had to work with Craig back there in the real world. She didn't want to quarrel.

How different her situation with Grant Bradley was, she thought. She could and did willingly cross swords with him . . . and came away invigorated.

"I don't get this place," Craig complained. "Who would be crazy enough to pay money to live like this?"

"Don't knock it until you've tried it. This is a lot more comfortable than what those Civil War re-enactors do. They live in military-style camps and refight famous battles. And then there's that organization that recreates Renaissance society. Or is it medieval? Knights and kingdoms and such. Anyway, they camp out too."

She'd always thought it might be fun to play at living in another century for a short period of time. She was certainly getting her wish!

"You couldn't get a penny out of me to stay here," Craig said.

That, Nessa mused, was a pity. She had a feeling her assistant's initiation into the nineteenth century had only just begun. Tomorrow the animals arrived. A horse, two milk cows, chickens, goats, and at least one pig. And Craig was no longer Craig, but Jake the farmhand. She considered reminding him of that, then decided he deserved whatever happened to him. No one had asked him to butt in.

"Damn, it's cold in here," he muttered.

"So start a fire." She gestured toward the hearth. The once-open fireplace had been closed off and a gleaming black cast-iron parlor stove installed. The sight of neatly stacked firewood next to it reminded her of the scene she'd come upon in the barn only a little more than an hour earlier. The memory momentarily erased her own need for greater warmth.

Silence settled over the sitting room, broken only by the ticking of the grandfather clock standing in one corner. Craig looked at her, at the woodstove, and back at her again. "I don't know how to start a fire."

Why didn't it surprise her that he'd never been a Boy Scout? "Looks like you'll have to learn, or find another way to warm up."

The gleam in his eyes startled her. She hadn't meant to be anything but sarcastic, but it was obvious Craig had other ideas. His one arm circled her shoulders while his free hand lightly touched her jaw. "I know this Jake character is supposed to sleep in the barn," he whispered, "but I don't have to. I could—"

A loud throat-clearing sound cut off what he'd

been about to suggest. Thank goodness! Craig jerked away from her as fast as any kid caught with his hand in the candy jar.

Nessa's relief faded in the next instant, when she saw who stood in the archway between the sitting and dining rooms. Grant Bradley had come in through the kitchen and slid pocket doors silently apart, giving her no warning of his presence until he chose to announce himself.

She wondered how much of their conversation he'd overheard.

He was scowling at the two of them, looking angry, Nessa thought. No. Not just angry. Jealous? She smiled to herself. Not likely. Now *there* was a case of imagination running away with her!

Their eyes locked and he seemed about to speak, but the moment was lost when the others arrived, all of them in costume now and eager to get started with the week's activities.

"You got something going with that guy?" Craig asked her in a whisper.

"I only met him today," she said.

"He seems to think he's got a claim on you."

Grant *was* still glowering at them, she noticed, almost as if he was trying to warn Craig off. Belatedly, an explanation occurred to her. "It isn't me he's upset with," she whispered. "It's the part I'm playing. Katie Westbrook. Remember? His character, Simon Hanlon, is in love with her. That's why he's acting so upset. Simon just caught his

Katie in a compromising position with the hired help."

Craig didn't look convinced.

After supper, and primarily for Craig Seton's benefit, Grant began the evening's planned seminar and organizational session by explaining once again that assigned roles had to be maintained except when participants were researching primary sources available on the premises.

"That means," he emphasized, "you answer to another name and live as much as possible as that person would have a hundred years ago. No wristwatches, cigarettes, or flashlights are allowed. About the only concessions we're making to modern times, and only for health reasons, are the additions of window screens, toilet paper, and sleeping bags."

Seton nodded, but he seemed more interested in watching Nessa than in paying attention to the information Grant was trying to give him. Hank wasn't much more receptive, and Mary Ellen, who had brought a large mending basket with her into the sitting room, appeared to be completely absorbed in her attempt to darn a sock. Jason, a fellow Sidwell professor who'd been known to ramble on endlessly about his own pet subjects, had a look of resignation on his face.

Grant glanced at one of the three-by-five cards

he held. "Participants will pay roughly the same amount they'd pay to stay in a motel."

Nessa made a note of that on the pad she'd propped on one knee. She was, he noticed with favor, writing with a pencil, not a felt-tip or some other modern version of a pen. They'd advanced from quills to fountain pens by 1890, but not much further.

His three-by-five cards were an anomaly he hoped no one would notice, a compromise he'd made for his own convenience. At least they were less intrusive than a computer printout.

"The Westbrook Farm project is modeled on a program developed by a National Endowment for the Humanities grant more than twenty years ago," he continued. "Summer sessions will run from Sunday afternoon until the following Sunday morning. A shorter live-in for families with children may be added later. Next fall we'll open to public schools, grades three through twelve, for field trips."

As Grant persevered with his planned presentation, the rough equivalent of the talk he'd give to participants on the first night of each live-in, he was keenly aware that he was boring Craig Seton. The man's eyes glazed over less than ten minutes into the lecture. Perversely, Grant decided to expand his remarks. He had little sympathy for someone who'd horned in where he hadn't been invited.

His glance strayed to Nessa more than once

during the next hour. Although she paid attention and took the occasional note, he couldn't help but be a bit hurt when he noticed she'd shifted the balance of her interest to Mary Ellen. His assistant's effort at darning was not going well. It was obvious no one had ever taught the younger woman how to go about it. Instead of one hole in the heel, there were now several, interspersed with interlaced threads.

Grant was thinking he'd have to ask Bea to give Mary Ellen lessons, when Nessa reached over and took charge of the endeavor. With practiced stitches, she quickly completed the task. For a moment Grant lost his train of thought. The ability to darn socks was not a skill he'd ever have expected a modern woman like Ms. Dare to possess. That she did frankly astonished him.

"Do you knit too?" he asked, temporarily abandoning his notecards.

She looked up at him, startled, then down at the wooden darning egg in her hand. "Ah, no."

"Crochet? Tat?"

"I darn," she said, sounding a little defensive. "And I know how to braid a rug. And I suppose if we had a sewing machine here, I could manage to operate one of those."

"Sewing by hand was still prized in 1890," Mary Ellen said. She seemed miffed at being outshone. "Besides, the Westbrooks had no electricity for a sewing machine."

"Actually," Grant corrected her, "there is an

old Singer in the attic, the model operated by a foot pedal. I'll bring it down if you like."

"Don't bother on my account," Nessa said. "I have plenty to keep me busy without making my own clothes."

Grant looked down at his cards, shuffling them a bit to cover the fact that he couldn't make sense of Vanessa Dare. Nessa sewing her own clothing? Braiding rugs? Darning? Not hobbies that fit the image he had of her. With a mental shrug, he was about to resume his monologue when the grandfather clock struck nine.

"Bedtime for the typical farmer," he announced instead. "Get a good night's sleep, everyone. Tomorrow's agenda includes such living history experiences as baking bread from scratch and learning to use a mowing scythe to cut grass."

FOUR

Nessa's bedroom was chilly, the bed more so, in spite of the warming pan she'd used on the sheets before crawling between them. The weather forecast she'd seen prior to leaving home had warned of temperatures dipping into the twenties that night, though the coming week was supposed to be less frigid. By morning she expected to find ice in the china pitcher Mary Ellen had filled with water and left on the washstand.

Shivering at the thought, Nessa rolled herself up in her thick wool blankets and flipped the corner of one of them over her nose. In a few minutes, she knew she'd be warm enough to fall asleep.

In the meantime, she couldn't help but recall how much more quickly beds heated up with more than one person in them. She had plenty of pleasant memories of how well that method worked. The three of them had often curled together like puppies to share body heat.

They'd had to sleep together for warmth as kids, she and her two older sisters. They couldn't afford to leave the thermostat turned up very high at night, and the winter nights got cold on the shore of Lake Erie. When she'd been growing up in Buffalo, Nessa's family hadn't been able to afford electric blankets either. Heck, sometimes they couldn't pay the electric bill at all. Their power had been shut off more than once.

She snuggled deeper into her cocoon of blankets and let her mind drift. Back then, they'd always had indoor plumbing, though it hadn't necessarily been in good repair. Getting the slumlord who owned their building to do anything about it—well, she'd made inroads there as an adult, as a reporter. She hadn't wanted a career as a crusader, or even as an investigative journalist, but she'd done some good work before moving on. She'd earned the right to pamper herself.

Her sisters had made successes of themselves too. The three of them together had made sure their mother, who'd had to work all her life at minimum wage, was able to enjoy a comfortable and carefree early retirement.

She really had to visit Ginny and Ronnie soon. It had been too long. As kids, they'd been inseparable. And always laughing. Teachers had called them the giggle sisters. They'd even giggled in bed on cold nights.

Their mother had taught them that a sense of humor was a survival tool. Ginny insisted it was also a way to judge men. A sort of litmus test for compatibility. She maintained that she'd known the man who was now her husband was the one for her the night their bed collapsed while they were making love. Their mutual response had been in three parts. Pause. Finish what they'd been doing. Collapse in gales of mirth.

Not the worst way to pick a mate, Nessa supposed. On the edge of sleep, her mind conjured up a picture of Grant Bradley in bed with her. She could all too easily imagine the two of them there, visualize making love together.

Where she had difficulty was hearing them share laughter.

Grant woke early. He'd slept like a log. He always did in the country, even when the weather was cold. As he'd told Nessa the day before, he wasn't going to risk anyone's health for the sake of authenticity. The rough-looking hired hands' bedroom in the barn was well insulated, and so were the sleeping bags he and Craig had spread atop two of the four beds.

The beds themselves were historically accurate, of course, made of large side timbers with holes bored into them for the ropes that took the place of bedsprings. Grant had used ninety feet of rope for each one. He'd secured the webbing with wedges to make it taut enough to hold a straw mattress and his own weight.

A low groan from the other side of the room drew his attention to Craig Seton. Grant wasn't sure what to make of Nessa's assistant. Or of their relationship.

None of your business, he told himself. Because Hank controlled the purse strings on this project, Grant had been stuck with Nessa and Hank himself, and now this uneducated amateur had been added to the mix.

According to Hank, Craig Seton had asked to be included because Nessa's claim that she'd be able to handle making the documentary by herself was exaggerated. Seton insisted she'd need help, and he'd offered to provide it. Grant wasn't convinced Seton's claim was true. Nessa seemed pretty proficient at whatever she did. But if she didn't require Seton's assistance, that left open the question of why a man with such an obvious lack of interest in history had turned up there determined to stay.

"There's water on the washstand," he said as Seton reluctantly climbed out of his sleeping bag, wincing as his bare feet touched the cold floorboards.

Seton hadn't been very talkative the previous night. He'd seemed a bit shell-shocked during a meal cooked on a woodstove and an evening in a sitting room lit only by kerosene lamps that produced a smoky, torchlike glow. He'd been almost pathetically grateful for the sleeping bag after they'd found their way from the house to the barn with the aid of a lantern instead of a flashlight.

"There's ice on top of this water," Seton complained in a sleep-fogged voice.

"So break it." Grant squinted into the mirror above the room's second washstand. No help for it. He needed a shave. He removed his recently sharpened razor from its case, mixed a little soap in a cup, and began the laborious process.

"Where's the outlet?" Seton asked. Grant had heard no sounds of ice breaking or cold water being sloshed on a face.

"No outlets," Grant reminded him. In the mirror, he could see the other man behind him. Seton was holding an electric razor in one hand and looking confused. Obviously, nothing Grant had said the night before had penetrated his thick skull. He'd have to dumb down his lectures from now on. Make sure there were no misunderstandings. The prospect annoyed him, but what choice did he have? He was stuck with Craig Seton's company, and he'd have to make the best of it.

"I'll teach you how to use this, if you like," he offered, flourishing his blade.

Seton swallowed convulsively and looked appalled by the idea. Probably afraid he'd slip and slit his own throat. Grant supposed he couldn't blame the fellow. Seton was out of his element, and Grant himself had only learned to be proficient at shaving with a straight razor by dint of long and painful practice.

"Maybe I'll grow a beard," Seton muttered.

Grant continued to remove stubble with long, smooth strokes, peripherally aware of the other man getting dressed and combing his hair. Seton kept a wary eye on what Grant was doing too.

"Give you odds that Nessa's going to want to film that," the other man suddenly said.

The image of her watching him shave startled Grant and made his hand unsteady. He nicked his chin as a result. Cursing silently, he stanched the trickle of blood.

Vanessa Dare was a problem, he thought grimly. She didn't even have to be in the same room to distract him.

When Nessa strolled into the big, old-fashioned kitchen, fresh from the best night's sleep she'd had in ages, she found Mary Ellen already there preparing breakfast. In readiness to start work, Nessa had dressed in blue jeans and a heavy cable-knit sweater. She'd also tucked a pair of gloves into her back pocket.

"That heat feels good," she said, indicating the cookstove, a range with six lids and a large oven. The moment she'd left her cocoon of blankets, she'd begun to shiver. Breaking ice to get to wash water was not her idea of a fun way to start the day. Did wake one up fast, though.

"You'll think it's too hot in a couple of minutes," Mary Ellen warned her. "We've been spoiled by central heating. Stand in front of this and your bosom cooks while your butt freezes."

"I don't suppose the professor is going to compromise on that one."

Mary Ellen laughed. "Not a chance." She had her supplies laid out on a large dresser next to the stove. It had a built-in flour bin and sifter and to one side was what appeared to be a dumbwaiter. Nessa wasn't sure where it would go. She had yet to explore all of the second floor.

"Can I give you a hand with anything?" The previous night, Mary Ellen had insisted on doing everything herself, to get a feel for it, she'd said. Nessa hadn't objected, but now she felt a little guilty, guessing how much work had been involved.

"If you want coffee, you can start that," Mary Ellen said, indicating a camp-style coffeepot sitting on the drainboard beside a slate sink.

A hand pump seemed to be the only means of obtaining water. Seeing no other way to coax it into flowing, Nessa put both hands on the pump handle and pushed. It took an effort to get it to move, but she persevered. Down. Down. Down. But no water came out. She tried again. Nothing.

"You have to prime it," said a deep voice. Grant.

Whirling around, Nessa glared at him. "Can't

you make a little noise when you come into a room? You're forever creeping up on me."

He lifted an eyebrow at that exaggeration, then ignored her complaint. Using a small container of water set aside for that purpose, he showed her how to get the pump going. His hands shadowed hers as they worked the handle together. He stood directly behind her, almost touching but not quite. She was very aware of every inch of him, especially when he took away the coffeepot she'd just picked up and handed her an ordinary pan.

"Heat water in this, then pour it over the grounds. This is a drip pot."

"Thank you." She grimaced when she heard how breathless she sounded and put the pan on top of the stove with a little more force than necessary.

"Anytime."

"We have a spring room too," Mary Ellen said, indicating a door. "The clever folks who built this place put it right over a spring. Water flows through there and is captured in a barrel. You can use a dipper to get it out."

"So I didn't need the pump?"

"Nope." Mary Ellen grinned at her, but her eyes had a slightly malicious glint. "Cheer up. He could have suckered you into going outside and drawing water direct from the well with a bucket. That'll get your juices flowing first thing in the morning!"

Nessa sat down in a slat-backed rocker to wait for the water to boil. She was already steaming, but she didn't say a word, just listened as Grant and Mary Ellen discussed their plans for the day.

Ever alert for opportunities for taping, she eavesdropped openly and gradually forgot her pique at Grant. The arrival of the animals ought to provide some interesting footage, she thought.

Her mind was soon preoccupied with ideas for the documentary. She was not concentrating fully on what she was doing when the water boiled and she began to pour it over the coffee grounds. She used a folded towel to lift the pan off the stove, oven mitts being too modern, but she put her bare hand on the side of the coffeepot to steady it as she transferred the steaming liquid. Her fingers jerked at the sudden rush of heat against metal, knocking the container to one side. A dollop of hot water splashed onto the back of her hand.

At the small, wounded sound she made, both Grant and Mary Ellen hurried to her side. "It's nothing," she said, lifting the burned skin to her mouth.

But Grant seized her hand and examined the red patch for himself. "Put it under cold water," he ordered. "I'll only be a minute."

With Mary Ellen to operate the pump, Nessa obeyed. "It's not serious," she told the other woman.

"No sense in taking chances."

Grant returned seconds later with a very modern looking first-aid kit. Nessa felt a rush of relief that left her a bit light-headed. Instead of grumbling at him, she found herself using a teasing tone of voice. "Why, Professor," she murmured, "surely this isn't authentic."

"Come out onto the stoop where the light's better."

She thought the light was perfectly fine in the kitchen, but she didn't argue with him. Blotting the water with a clean, dry towel, she followed him.

The small back porch looked over fields on the east side of the farm. There had been hoarfrost on the ground earlier, but now that the sun had risen, it was rapidly vanishing. Nessa felt warmer there than she had inside.

Or maybe it was just because of the company. Grant dabbed first-aid cream on the back of her hand using long, slow, sensuous strokes that had her heart rate accelerating and her breath coming in short gulps.

"Good as new," he murmured, releasing her to put the cap back on the tube.

"Thank you." Nessa knew she sounded breathless again. They'd already played this scene. Grant must think she was a helpless—what was the word? She flashed on a Regency romance she'd once read. Ninnyhammer. That was it. Not quite the right period, but close enough.

She tried to focus on the view, to give herself a moment to recover. An oddly charged atmosphere seemed to engulf them, one she did not care to examine too closely. She stared at the fenced-in paddocks and outbuildings instead.

"I know that's the barn," she said. Stairs on one side led to the hired hands' room. "What are the others?"

"The small shed nearest this door from the kitchen is the washroom for doing laundry. Over there are the pigsty and chicken coop." He removed his glasses and pointed with them.

Farsighted, Nessa concluded as she looked in the direction he indicated. He probably wore the glasses for reading and forgot to take them off. Together they watched a hardy robin optimistically attack a muddy hump of ground in the shade next to the chicken coop.

"That's the smokehouse on the other side of the barn. You already know about the three-hole privy."

She nodded. It was about twenty yards from the northwest corner of the house, at the end of a flagstone walk.

"Then down by the pond there's a boathouse and an icehouse. Ice was once harvested every winter for use all year round. Our perishable food is stored in ice boxes in the spring room, but for now the ice comes from the nearest supermarket."

With pleasure, Nessa noticed that the brown grass in the fields had new green shoots poking through it. The distant pond glimmered in the sun. And closer at hand, just at the edge of the dooryard near an empty watering trough, a few crocus stalks had forced their way up out of the still-frigid earth.

A sense of calm settled over her. This place was all she'd looked for. Here she could find both peace and productivity . . . as long as she did not allow herself to be distracted by the man standing next to her.

She turned to thank him for tending to her injury.

It was a mistake. The moment she looked into Grant Bradley's dark eyes, she realized she was in big trouble.

As a strong, sensual awareness washed through her, he smiled at her.

"You feel it too." There was a distinctly masculine satisfaction in his voice.

That should have infuriated her. Instead, she felt herself melt, her knees weakening, her thoughts scattering as he set his glasses on the porch railing so he could slide both hands up her arms and pull her closer. They continued their journey until he cupped her face with his palms.

She told herself she wasn't resisting only because it would have been undignified to struggle.

She lied.

Nessa tried to look away, but he caught her chin and lifted her head until their gazes once more locked. His lips came closer, brushing her mouth with feather lightness. Once. Twice.

The third time, she kissed him back.

If a touch had produced electrical sparks the day before, being kissed by him was akin to grabbing a live wire. Current surged through her, sending new energy to the tips of her toes, prickling her scalp, and setting off a throbbing in one crucial area halfway between.

By the time the first shock began to fade, Nessa had pressed herself close to the source of all those delicious sensations. He changed the angle of his mouth and sent another bolt of barely leashed lightning straight to her womb. If they'd been anyplace else, she might have let herself enjoy being kissed. But she couldn't quite forget where they were . . . or who might come upon them at any moment.

"This shouldn't be happening," she whispered.

"I know."

The next kiss was hotter, deeper, and more mind-boggling than anything Nessa had ever experienced. When she heard Grant's muffled groan, she knew he was no more immune to its power than she was.

"Oh, God," she whispered against his mouth. "What are we doing? This will never work."

"Are you sure?"

By the fifth kiss she was pressed against the door, his body aligned with hers. Pure want swept through her. Nessa forgot everything but the pleasure of their embrace. He seemed to know exactly how to tap into her most passionate depths.

Bemused, Nessa's brain began to provide graphic images. They would make love to each other in that big bed upstairs. And in the barn loft atop a bed of hay.

On the brink of suggesting they waste no more time on preliminaries, she heard a voice from inside the house. Insistent, annoying, and all too familiar, it abruptly brought her to her senses.

"Nessa? Where are you?" Craig was right on the other side of the door.

Jerked back to reality, Nessa began to struggle. Grant released her at once, but with obvious reluctance. Heat flooded into her face as she forced herself to meet his eyes. With an effort, she kept her voice steady as well. "This can't happen again."

He stepped away from her, his expression closed. His words were clipped and cold. "Certainly, Ms. Dare. We have a business arrangement. Nothing more."

"Right." So why did she feel so disappointed?

"Right," he repeated.

"Besides, for all I know, you're married and have a dozen kids."

He cleared his throat and put his glasses back on. "I'm not married, but the future of Westbrook Farm is as important to me as a baby's health is to its parents. I'm not about to do anything to threaten that."

"I'm a threat?" she murmured, confused.

A sardonic smile flickered across his hard features so swiftly, Nessa was sure she'd imagined it. "Oh, yes," he told her. "Most definitely. But I learn from sad experience. You're here for one reason and one reason only, Ms. Dare. You stick to your job, and I'll stick to mine. We'll both be happier that way."

FIVE

Stupid, stupid, stupid! Grant chastised himself. What had he thought he was doing that morning, hauling the woman into his arms and kissing her like that? Kissing her at all?

After what had happened with Corinne, he ought to have more sense. He'd trusted Corinne and look where he'd ended up. He had no idea how he'd dared banter so easily with a stranger like Nessa, let alone kiss her. His behavior had been idiotic, not to mention risky. Several hours after the incident on the back stoop, he was still astonished at his lack of control.

The lapses in judgment had started even earlier. From the moment they'd met, he'd been impulsive in what he'd said to her and how he'd acted. He couldn't understand it. Since Corinne, he'd gotten into the habit of behaving with a certain formality around women. All women. He'd found that his tendency to lecture helped keep females at a distance.

That ploy didn't seem to work with Vanessa Dare.

From the back entrance of the barn, he watched Nessa perch on the top railing of a fence and fiddle with her camera, intent on finding the perfect angle for a shot of Doug Roper showing Seton how to use a walking plow. The plan was to till the soil and plant a small garden during this weeklong stay, even though it was a bit soon to sow most crops.

It had also been too early in the year to mow the field first. Probably just as well, Grant decided. If Seton was spooked by a straight razor, Grant would hate to see him try to handle a scythe.

Nessa, on the other hand, hadn't needed to be shown how to knead dough for the day's bread, now rising in the kitchen. She'd seemed to enjoy helping out, even after that unfortunate business with the scalding water.

Grant wanted to think Nessa was exactly what she appeared to be, open and honest, but he didn't dare. He hadn't forgotten the hard lesson he'd learned about trusting women, especially those who could appear to be something they weren't.

He'd already been far too open with her. He was going to have to quell that irrational impulse he kept feeling to joke with her, to tease her. He didn't even want to think about the way he reacted to her physically, responding to her every movement, every touch, with a teenager's libido.

They'd agreed neither one of them wanted more than a professional association. He was determined to stick to that bargain . . . even if it killed him.

"She seems to know what she's doing," Bea Roper said as she came up beside him. The top of her head was level with his shoulder, and she was nearly as wide as she was high, a marked contrast to her husband, who was a tall, thin, rawboned fellow with a long, homely face.

"I hope so," Grant said. "Hank has plans to sell copies of her documentary as well as use it for promotional purposes." He wasn't much interested in the business end of things. As long as his dream could be realized, he'd make a deal with the devil.

Maybe he already had.

"Nice looking too."

"Don't start, Bea." She was one of the people he loved best in the world, but she did have a tendency to try to rearrange people's lives.

"Me? Meddle? Heaven forbid! Doug and I have enough to contend with settling in here. Looks like you have competition, anyway." Bea nodded her graying head in Craig's direction.

"I wish I knew why he really came here."

"To keep an eye on Ms. Dare. He watches her all the time. Haven't you noticed?"

Grant had seen Seton with his arms around

Nessa on the sofa the previous afternoon. And he had felt—what? Envy? He tried to tell himself that was impossible. He barely knew the woman, had known her even less well then. Chemistry aside, he had no basis for having feelings of any kind toward her.

"I'd like a close-up," Nessa called, drawing his attention back to her. She walked through the gate and crossed the lumpy, newly disturbed earth to the two men and the horse.

Unlike Craig, she showed no trepidation around the big animal, though as soon as she came close with the camera he shied away. She produced an apple from one of the tote bags she always seemed to have at hand when she was working and let him lip it off her palm.

Nessa chatted easily with Doug Roper, too, which surprised Grant. Doug had spent his entire life doing research in the field of animal husbandry and was usually shy around strangers. Recently retired, he regarded his stint at Westbrook Farm as caretaker and re-enactor as a vacation, although he'd already started lobbying for the installation of a modern shower somewhere on the premises.

"Let's join them," Bea suggested. "I need to find out when it will be convenient to break for lunch. Dinner, I mean. That's the one thing I have trouble getting used to, these big meals in the middle of the day."

Grant let her lead him toward Nessa, mild as a

lamb going to the slaughter. He didn't try to stop himself from staring, either, when she handed Craig her camera in order to dust her hands on her jeans. The swift, economical movements drew his gaze to her thighs, lovingly shaped by denim. When she slipped a pair of gloves out of her back pocket, he couldn't help but notice more delightful curves.

Stupid, stupid, stupid, he thought again. He had things to do elsewhere. He didn't need to cross the field and stand next to her, inhaling the scent of her soap along with the rich smell of fresh-turned earth.

But he did.

"They need names too," Nessa was saying. She was looking toward the pasture where the two cows had been set loose to graze. "Old Bossie, or some such."

"My mother used to talk about the pair of oxen they had on her parents' place when she was a girl," Doug said. "We ought to have oxen here, Grant."

"I plan on it. Eventually."

Satisfied with Grant's answer, Doug turned back to Nessa. "Buck and Bill, Ma's animals were called."

Nessa grinned. "So farm animals may not have been pets, but they weren't just numbers, either." She ran a hand over the horse's neck. "What do you think, boy?"

"He thinks he likes Bossie," Bea said. "What about the other cow?"

"Elsie," Doug decided. "Elsie and Bossie."

"Let me guess," Grant said. "You've already named the horse."

"Of course," Nessa replied. "There was only one possible choice." A mischievous smile lit her entire face.

"Mr. Ed?" In spite of his reservations, he found himself wanting to join in the spirit of fun already infecting the others.

Nessa shook her head. "His name is Not-a-Cow."

Taken aback, Grant started to protest, but before he could do more than sputter, Nessa cut him off.

"Oh, no, Professor. No lectures, please! I know there are thousands of names more suitable, and you can probably rattle off every one of them, together with the first date each appeared in the annals of farm life, but won't you humor me, just this once?"

She fluttered her eyelashes at him, outrageous woman.

"Is that a smile?" she asked, pretending to be amazed by the sight.

It hadn't been, but it was now. He couldn't help responding to her. Her teasing should have annoyed him. Instead he had to work hard not to laugh out loud, especially when she insisted on also naming the chickens and the pig.

The tight coil of tension in his chest, a symptom he'd been living with for years, slowly began to loosen. She made him feel younger. Carefree. It was a dangerously seductive sensation.

Their second evening at Westbrook Farm, the entire company gathered again in the sitting room after supper, everyone except Hank Gilbert. He'd left at noon, since he had to be in court early the next morning to plead a case. He planned to come back as soon as he could wrap it up.

Nessa was feeling very mellow. The day's work had gone well.

Contentment vanished, however, when Jason took out a pipe and began tamping in tobacco. He hadn't smoked before, and Nessa had been hoping he'd quit. Apparently not. She hated to make a fuss, but she refused to inhale secondhand smoke.

"Must you?" Bea asked in a quelling voice, though whether as "Nathan's mother" or herself, Nessa couldn't tell.

Jason struck a match. "Better than a cheroot. I understand gentlemen were fond of those in Nathan's day."

"There's no evidence Nathan smoked anything," Bea said.

"None he didn't."

Grant cut short the debate with a quiet reminder. "That pipe's a fire hazard."

"And lamps and woodstoves aren't?" Jason looked incredulous.

"How are you getting around regulations on safety?" Nessa asked. "Doesn't this place have to pass some kind of inspection if it's to open as a boarding house?"

"It was a farm and a boarding house in the last century. In this one it's a museum."

"There must still be regulations. Codes." She already knew Grant was prepared to compromise when safety was the issue. He had on the matter of corsets. She'd learned more about the dangers of wearing those from Mary Ellen. Seemed they compressed the internal organs, doing untold damage. And some women, horrific as it sounded, had actually gone to surgeons to have their float-ing ribs removed under primitive operating room conditions in order to obtain an even smaller waist.

"There are both smoke alarms and fire extin-guishers on the premises," Grant said. "And I have a cellular phone."

That made at least three, Nessa realized, with hers and Craig's. Hers was buried in the bottom of the standing wardrobe in her room.

Grant suggested a quick tour, during which he would show them where each safety device had been cleverly concealed. He started with the smoke alarm and fire extinguisher hidden in the downstairs bedroom Bea and Doug were using.

As they covered the rest of the building at a

rapid pace, Nessa made plans to come back and shoot a bit of every room. At the same time, she began to compose the accompanying narration in her head: *Here is the "addition" the Westbrooks added in 1880, during the boom in the popularity of farm/ boarding houses in the area. A large hotel opened in Luzon in 1891, but prior to that vacationers who wanted to escape New York City's summertime heat and crowding flocked in droves to places like this one. Primitive conditions didn't bother them. Life in the city wasn't much more luxurious.*

The addition was a square block connected to the first floor of the original farmhouse by two doors, one from the spring room and the other from the small "writing room," so named because boarders went there to write letters home. A large summer dining room filled with long tables dominated the lower level of the addition. Upstairs were six bedrooms which, together with five bedrooms of various sizes on the second floor of the main house, could sleep up to forty people. Grant had mentioned the night before that the Westbrooks themselves sometimes camped out in the attic, or moved to the barn during the high season in July and August, to make room for paying customers.

Grant led the group back into the upstairs hall of the main house, reached by way of yet another connecting door. "There's one more fire extinguisher in there," he said, indicating a room Nessa hadn't noticed before. It was tucked away in an obscure corner that she thought must be just above the kitchen. Above the dumbwaiter she'd noticed that morning.

"What else is in there?" she asked, suddenly curious.

"Oh, that's the bathroom," Mary Ellen said.

Nessa and Craig rounded on her in unison. "What?"

"Literally," Grant warned. He opened the door to reveal a small cubicle furnished with a tub and a washstand. "Water heated in the kitchen can be put in buckets and hoisted upstairs in the dumbwaiter."

"You rat," Nessa said, glaring at Grant. "I could have had a nice, hot soak before supper instead of sluicing off the dirt with cold water."

"Think of it this way," Grant answered. "Now you have something to look forward to."

Their eyes locked. His glasses did nothing to filter the desire she saw smoldering in his. The air between them began to sizzle, and Nessa flashed on a vivid image of herself soaking in that tub.

She was naked in the fantasy, and she was not alone.

Grant blinked, dispelling her illusion. She looked quickly away, only to focus on Mary Ellen's annoyed expression.

"Well, now that everyone is reassured about safety," Grant said, "shall we return to business?"

Oblivious to the daggers his assistant was shooting with her eyes at his videographer, he herded them downstairs and into the sitting room. As he had the previous night, he assumed his professorial role.

"These are some of the albums, ledgers, autograph books, and letters found here in the house," he announced. "They will help flesh out the characters of the Westbrooks, their friends, and their summer boarders. Remember, please, that anything after 1890 is to be ignored."

As he droned on, albeit in a pleasant baritone, Nessa shifted position, trying to get comfortable on cushions made of fabric so prickly, it was capable of jabbing right through layers of cashmere and cotton to bare skin. She fervently hoped this speech wasn't going to last too long.

Lighten up a little, she thought, directing the command at Grant. He was addressing the group as he would lecture freshmen in a required course. He seemed to be playing to the lowest common denominator of intelligence, too, though she supposed she couldn't blame him given Craig's poor showing during the day.

She bit back a smile, remembering her assistant's chagrin when he'd managed to take the cows out to pasture without incident, then stepped right into the middle of a fresh patty on his way back to the barn. Nessa had heard the squish from ten feet away. They'd probably heard Craig cussing all the way to Luzon. "It looked like a solid clump of mud," he'd complained as he'd tried in vain to clean the sole of one expensive shoe by scraping it on the ground.

The grandfather clock in the corner bonged the quarter hour. Grant continued to drone. Nessa made a mental note not to let him write any of the narration for the documentary. He obviously had a passionate interest in every detail of late nineteenth-century life, but very few people, even those who might want to come and experience it for a week, could share the intense fascination he exhibited.

When he began to summarize the political situation in 1890, Nessa's gaze drifted from his face to the windows at his back. She couldn't see anything now, since it was dark, but she knew she could use that view in daylight. It was just loaded with bucolic charm. Pastoral. Even romantic. She'd include lots of shots of the professor too. As long as he didn't open his mouth and start lecturing, he'd be a real draw for the ladies.

"How did the Westbrooks pass their evenings?" she asked, cutting into his monologue. Enough was enough. She wasn't that interested in "today's" politics.

Grant pinned her with his gaze, obviously annoyed. She stared back, defiant. If he was going to prose on and on, he might as well offer information that would be useful to her. After a moment, he seemed to realize that.

"They played the piano and sang. Katie kept a scrapbook. Tunis recorded events in a daybook."

"A diary?" Now that had potential

"See for yourself." He extracted a thin, leather-bound volume from the pile of materials at his side and passed it to her. "Read any page. Aloud, please."

What is this? she wondered. *A reading exercise?* But she complied, selecting an early entry.

"June 27, 1890. A heavy rain. The streams were very high from 6 o'clock until 7. It rained very hard until 8. Fell 4 inches. The streams were higher than they had been in 30 years. It took out many bridges, done damage to mill & dam, washed roads. The Arch Bridge was undermined at the lower end and at Gird's Tannery went off. Also the wooden bridge at Luzon & both of them near Jim Schoonmaker's. The C.T. Kilbourne mill was badly impaired. Most of them at Bushville went off and many others in town."

"That's the kind of material," Grant said, "that meticulous detail, that can be expanded from a mere monograph into an entire book on nineteenth-century life. The scholar investigates other sources to confirm these details. Checks records. Does background research on all the people and places mentioned."

Nessa had to admit that learning history this way was much more interesting than reading a textbook. "So," she said, "what you're doing is a lot like detective work."

Her observation seemed to please him, but Mary Ellen interrupted before he could respond. "There are domestic details in the daybooks too.

Wasn't there a note on wallpapering the bedroom?"

She held her hand out for the book, and Nessa passed it over. Grant sent his assistant an approving look.

"Yes. Here it is," Mary Ellen said. "*March 27-8, 1890. Edward and Walter Randall papered our sitting room and bedroom. It cost $3.30 for the work and $2.90 for the paper.* Did you know they also used to paper the inside of the outhouses in the old days? They thought that might make using them more pleasant for the boarders."

"There's probably a research project in that for you," Grant mused. "If you want to focus on nineteenth-century sanitation."

"I want to focus on matters of interest to women," Mary Ellen told him earnestly. "How the house was decorated. What they wore."

"You need an original topic for your dissertation," he reminded her.

"I'll take the maidservant's view."

Mary Ellen was decked out, Nessa supposed, in what the well-dressed domestic servant of the 1890s must have worn. The rust-colored dress had at least two dozen tiny buttons up the back, and the big white apron she wore over it, though tied at the waist, was also fastened by buttons at the shoulders. She had to be a contortionist if she'd done those up on her own.

Or might she have had help?

Unable to stop herself, Nessa glanced at Grant.

"You'd do better to focus on just one aspect of that," he said.

"On underwear, perhaps." Nessa meant to be sarcastic, but teacher and student alike looked taken with the idea.

"Perfect," Mary Ellen said. "And I know just where to start. I was looking at a copy of an 1890 mail-order catalog the other day. It offered the most marvelous things for sale. A bustle that resembled half a birdcage fastened onto the back end of a garter belt. And a 'Sahlin Waist Front Distender' guaranteed to give a full bust and small waist effect when worn under full front garments."

"Don't forget Zephyr Bosom Pads," Nessa put in.

They both turned to stare at her.

"Hey! I know how to do research too. I did a show on breast implants. Zephyr Bosom Pads were a forerunner. They were apparently expanded with air to increase bust size."

"She's a gold mine of useless information," Craig muttered.

"How else do you think I come up with segments for my show?"

" 'Beware of Bran,' for instance?" Grant asked. He almost sounded as if he were teasing her.

Nessa gave him a hard look. At once his expression altered. Somber-faced, he fiddled with the lamp on the marble-topped table beside him, adjusting the flame beneath the frosted glass globe and running his fingers over the shiny brass stand.

She was seized by a sudden, vivid recollection of how those hands had felt moving on her arms, her face. To rid herself of that all-too-potent image, Nessa rushed into speech, hardly caring what she said so long as it covered up the sudden rush of emotions she felt.

"Did you know that dinosaur hunters in Wyoming discovered the remains of four previously unknown species of small mammals?" she blurted. "Scientists have nicknamed one of them the prehistoric mutant ninja chipmunk. It was a six-ounce furry meat eater with vicious fangs that preyed on other small swamp animals."

"And what else have you done shows on, dear?" Bea asked. She was smiling benignly, as if she suspected what Nessa was trying to hide with her babbling.

The possibility that she'd been transparent in her reaction to Grant left Nessa, uncharacteristically, at a loss for words. Fortunately, Craig answered for her. Any other time, she'd have resented his advocacy. For once she was only grateful.

"I don't usually like historical segments," he told Bea, "but there was one on this seaside resort in Israel. Archaeologists working there unearthed evidence of a fourth-century brothel, complete with an ancient version of a hot tub and a sign, written in Greek, that said 'Enter, enjoy, and . . .'"

"And what?" Mary Ellen asked.

Craig grinned. "That will forever be a mystery. The rest of the sign had broken off and crumbled to dust."

"Bummer."

Encouraged by the pretty young woman's interest, Craig kept going. "One of the most useful shows we've done was the one on common household dangers. Did you know that if you accidentally mix chlorine bleach and ammonia together you produce a toxic gas?"

"No fear of that here," Mary Ellen assured him, and launched into a description of the way she cleaned the stove and other items in the kitchen. Lysol disinfectant, it turned out, dated from 1889.

Show-off, Nessa thought, barely listening as Mary Ellen went on about sprinkling salt on the stove to remove dirt and using sand to scour pots. She did catch a tip about adding a teaspoon of kerosene to dishwater, though. Apparently, that was thought to prevent typhoid.

As Mary Ellen continued, Nessa's gaze kept straying to Grant. He didn't seem to be paying attention to his assistant's monologue either. He'd settled into one of the wing chairs, long legs stretched out in front of him. He was staring at his boots, but his mind was obviously far away.

Nessa watched him until he looked up, straight into her eyes. Immediately, the air between them began to sizzle. She ought to be getting used to this, she thought as her pulse rate raced and her breathing became constricted.

Reluctantly, she faced the truth. This particular chemical reaction was not unlike the result one got by mixing two incompatible household cleansers. Her automatic attraction to Grant Bradley rated all kinds of warning labels.

Hazardous.

Keep your distance.

Slippery when wet.

SIX

Surprised to find the writing room occupied later that night, Grant hesitated in the doorway. It was well past ten, and he was making his final round to check the fires. A parlor stove similar to the one in the sitting room, though smaller, provided heat for the writing room. A single oil lamp gave off light, shedding wavering beams on the woman at the desk and the leather-bound volume open in front of her.

It was one of Tunis's daybooks, and Nessa seemed completely absorbed by it, proving to Grant what he had begun to suspect soon after meeting her. She was much more than just a pretty face. The words she used on camera were more likely her own than any scriptwriter's.

Seeing her thus, Grant was impressed by her diligence. And by her powers of concentration, since she gave no sign that she heard him. And by her elegance.

One leg crooked under her, she sat in the old wooden office chair, bent forward over the book. She still wore Katie's blue gown, into which she'd changed for supper. She might really have been a woman of the last century, he thought, right down to the guilty expression on her face when she looked up and saw him watching her.

"Did you know women weren't supposed to read newspapers for themselves in Victorian times?" he asked. "The men in their lives were afraid it might give them ideas."

"This isn't a newspaper," she said defensively. "And Katie obviously did read the papers. I was looking at her scrapbook earlier. It's full of clippings from the New York *World*."

"Have you found anything interesting in Tunis's daybook?"

"Nothing in particular. I was skimming through to see if it would spark any ideas for scenes to re-enact on tape."

He saw now that her small notebook sat on the desk too. Several lines had been scribbled on the top page, but he could not read what they said from the doorway. He came into the room.

"Most of what Tunis recorded is the same sort of thing we were reading aloud a few hours ago," she said.

"He was an old gossip. He reported everything that went on in his neighborhood. A good thing too. Modern historians would soon be out of business if people didn't yield to the urge to record details of everyday life."

Grant was close enough now to pick up her notebook and flip back through pages she'd filled with close-written words. Nessa stood and grabbed for it, but he easily evaded her, at least long enough to see that her notes covered such diverse aspects of her craft as audio effects, length of segments, camera angles, and lighting.

When she caught his elbow and tugged, he released her property, but not before he'd read the most recent notation. "What do you want to know about hammocks?" he asked.

"According to Tunis's daybook, the Westbrooks had one. Does it still exist?"

"It doesn't, but because of the references in the records and the popularity of hammocks at resorts of the period, I had two reproductions made. They're ready to be put up anytime."

Her face brightened instantly. "Wonderful."

Her hand was still on his arm, and they were standing very close together. The warmth of her fingers penetrated his coat sleeve. He looked at it, then up at her, and was in time to see awareness dawn. She backed away, withdrawing her hand as if it had been scalded again.

"I thought we agreed—"

"We did," he said. He heard the regret in his voice and suspected she had too.

"Just kidding around with each other is safer."

"Much."

"I enjoy talking with you, Grant. I admire what you're doing at Westbrook Farm. I know I'm an amateur when it comes to history, but I find myself hoping you'll come to consider me a colleague, at least for the rest of the time I'll be here."

Colleague?

No, he didn't think so. He'd had enough of colleagues. A coldness settled over him that had nothing to do with the fire dying in the stove or the rattle of the wind outside the window. He was in danger of letting Vanessa Dare slip through the barriers he'd built after Corinne's betrayal. Holding himself stiffly, he searched for words.

She obviously sensed his withdrawal, for a puzzled frown replaced her eager, hopeful expression. "If that's too much to ask . . ."

"I might manage friendship." He sounded grudging even to his own ears. "I don't need a partner."

"Friends, then." She turned away, gathering up the books and papers on the desk with more haste than grace. "Well, it's late. I'd best get to bed. See you in the morning."

And with that she was gone.

Friends? he repeated silently. There was an irony. He was far too attracted to her for simple friendship, and sometimes he liked her as well. But if there was one thing he'd learned to mistrust more than a woman from the media, it was a woman who expressed a desire to share in one of his projects.

If he had any sense at all, he'd stay as far away from Nessa as was humanly possible. And he'd keep his research notes under lock and key.

The next morning Grant was scowling as he watched Nessa prepare to tape a scene of a courting couple using Mary Ellen and Craig. Or rather Molly and Jake. What that had to do with serious historical study, he failed to comprehend, but when it came to the documentary, Hank had made it clear Vanessa Dare was in charge, not Grant.

Everyone else seemed to be enthusiastic, even Jason, who had helped string up the two huge, old-fashioned canvas hammocks decorated with fringe. When they were securely attached between conveniently placed shade trees, Jason tested one, Nessa the other. She flopped down full length, setting it swaying.

"This is great!" The sides of the hammock seemed to swallow her whole. "It's like being in a giant cradle with the sun and sky overhead."

Craig Seton came up beside her. "Shove over," he said. "These things were meant for two."

Nessa sat up, but to Grant's satisfaction, she hopped out of the hammock before Craig could join her, ordering Mary Ellen to take her place.

Grant watched for a few more minutes, then started to walk away. He turned back when he heard Mary Ellen's indignant screech. "He tried to put his hand up my skirt!"

Seton held both hands in front of him in mock surrender. "Jeez, it was an accident. Okay? You were squirming around, and my hand slipped."

"It slips again, buster, and I'll be charging you with sexual harassment."

Grant froze, a bitter taste filling his mouth. How easily women threw those words around, even Mary Ellen. He was suddenly very glad he'd been so circumspect around her. He'd seen the come-hither looks she occasionally sent his way and had long since decided to ignore them. He didn't need that kind of complication in his life.

He did not need to be around another woman who flung out unfounded charges at the drop of a hat.

Nessa waded into the fray, separating the two glaring combatants and giving both a lecture on professionalism. "You're supposed to be a couple from the late nineteenth century," she reminded them. "And back then no one knew what sexual harassment was. If he gets out of line, slap his face. That'll look just as good on tape as kissing and canoodling."

She went back to her camera, fiddled with it a moment, then made an exasperated sound. It took her a few seconds to change the battery that powered it. Then she was ready to go again. Mary

Ellen and Craig looked leery of each other, but they cooperated.

Before long, they actually seemed to be enjoying the "acting" and were going at it hot and heavy in the hammock. Then Mary Ellen hauled off and smacked him.

Craig sat up fast, holding the side of his face and looking at her in astonishment. It took Mary Ellen a moment to get free of the hammock, but once she was on the ground, she flounced off. Unfortunately, she forgot there was a second hammock strung between the two trees on that side. She ran right into it, and into Jason, who was lying in it.

"Hammock-hopping?" he asked, raising one eyebrow. He looked, Grant thought, like an overweight satyr.

"Cut," Nessa called. She was chuckling. The rest were laughing.

"None of you are taking this project seriously," Grant muttered. Not even Mary Ellen. He told himself that was the only reason he was annoyed. But was it? Irritation at his own overreaction propelled him forward. "Time to get back to work," he stated, striding to a point between the hammocks. "Molly. Jake. Don't you have chores?"

"You take life too seriously, Simon," Jason said, flopping back into his hammock. The only professionally trained actor among them, he slipped easily in and out of his character. "You aren't in line to inherit, you know. Me, now, I'm the oldest son. Mama's golden boy. Right?"

"Right, *Nathan*. But I've always believed you to be a hard worker."

Grant felt he was being baited, and it didn't cool his temper any to realize Nessa's camera was running. She was catching this exchange on tape. Rather than say more to Jason, he decided it was high time to follow his own advice.

"I'll be in the barn if anyone needs me," he said curtly. He walked away from Nessa without meeting her eyes and did not look back.

But he could hear what was said behind him. Jason abruptly dropped out of Nathan's persona to make a smart remark to Nessa.

"Possessed, I think," he said in a stage whisper. "Simon's spirit just moves in and takes over, in the best supernatural horror story tradition. I'd be careful if I were you. Who knows what Simon got up to with good old Katie."

"I gather you've known Grant for some time," Nessa said to Bea Roper a few hours later. She was back in costume, this time in Katie's second dress, which, according to Jason, was called a Mother Hubbard wrapper by the theater's wardrobe mistress. Made of bottle-green flannel, it had knife plaiting around the bottom, a plaited yoke, and a turned-down collar. It might not have a bustle, but the skirt was still voluminous, and there were just as many layers of undergarments beneath.

"I've known Grant all his life," Bea said as she stuck her bare arm into the oven to test how hot it was.

Participating, as she'd agreed to, in the daily life at Westbrook Farm, Nessa sat at the scrubbed pine kitchen table peeling potatoes.

"He's Doug's sister's boy," Bea added, pulling her arm back out and closing the oven door. "Too hot," she muttered. "I should be able to hold my arm in there for a count of twenty. A little sand sprinkled in the bottom ought to cool it enough to bake the bread." She went off to fetch some, leaving Nessa to her thoughts.

Bea was Grant's aunt? She wondered why he hadn't mentioned that detail. He seemed to show very little warmth toward her. Then Nessa smiled, divining the answer. Affection was for the twentieth century. In the nineteenth, this woman was Ella Westbrook, Simon Hanlon's much despised once-and-future mother-in-law.

Grant did try to stay in character, Nessa mused. Much more so than anyone else, although he didn't usually bother to pretend to be Simon when he was with her. He should have been courting Katie, but he acted as if he resented being attracted to Nessa. She wasn't sure whether to be relieved or disappointed by his attitude.

A chill passed through her as she remembered Jason's comment earlier in the day. What foolishness. Grant wasn't possessed, just dedicated. She admired that quality.

Truth be told, she admired quite a lot about Professor Grant Bradley. His vision. His intellect. All the hard work he'd put into restoring this place. She had yet to discover any detail he'd overlooked. In those rare instances where he'd had to compromise, for the sake of safety or health, every detail had been carefully thought out and the appearance of authenticity retained.

She hadn't had time before coming to Westbrook Farm to do more than a surface check of Grant's credentials, but he seemed to be well respected in the academic community. He certainly enjoyed the loyalty and support of his longtime friend Hank, even if the two did sometimes disagree on specifics.

Depositing another skinned potato in the bowl in her lap, Nessa idly wondered if the man she was so drawn to on a physical level was the real Grant Bradley, or Simon Hanlon, or some combination of the two.

What did it matter? She was there on business. It made no sense to get involved with someone she'd have no reason to see again after this week. They led very different lives. Hers was back home, clear on the other side of the state. He was firmly ensconced at Sidwell College. And at the Westbrook Farm project.

"Has Grant always been so single-minded?"

she asked when Bea returned from the spring room with a handful of sand.

Bea's first answer was a snort of laughter. Then, once she was satisfied with her ministrations to the oven, she said, "He's got tunnel vision, that boy does. Sometimes it's a good thing. Sometimes not."

"How not?"

"Well, take women, for example."

Nessa waited, unsure she wanted to hear this.

"One bad experience," Bea said, "and he's ready to write off the entire sex. Of course it was a very bad experience, no doubting that, but still . . ." Her voice trailed off as she regarded Nessa with a speculative gaze.

"You're saying there's some specific reason he doesn't trust women?" Someone had hurt him, soured him on love. Or was Bea exaggerating?

"Not attractive ones," Bea answered. "And not if they have anything to do with the media." There was a sparkle in the other woman's eyes before she turned away to slide the first of six bread pans into the oven.

Intrigued in spite of her reservations, Nessa tried to pump Bea for more information.

"You'll have to ask Grant himself if you want to know more," was all Bea said, however. "He seems to have a weak spot where you're concerned. Haven't seen that in a coon's age. Not since Corinne accused him of—" She broke off without finishing the sentence. Deliberately, Nessa thought.

"Of?"

"No, not another word."

Suddenly reminded of the odd look she'd seen on Grant's face earlier in the day, when Mary Ellen threatened Craig with sexual harassment, Nessa bent over her work. A powerful emotion had shown there, though briefly. At the time, she'd believed it was anger and had wondered if he had stronger feelings for Mary Ellen than she'd supposed. Now she wasn't so sure.

Her knife sliced steadily, adding to the pile of potato skins. What did it matter? Hadn't she just rationalized that getting involved with Grant was a bad idea? She was there to make a documentary, then she would return home and continue to build her new career behind the camera. She planned to keep her old job for a while longer, but she hoped to make a reputation with this new work. As soon as possible, she'd go independent, form her own production company to operate from the base she'd spent the last ten years establishing in the community where she did her show.

There was no room in that scenario for a long-distance romance. No room for any romance at all. She was going to be far too busy.

"You should get him to talk to you," Bea said.

"You know, *Mother*," Nessa said, willing to use her role as Katie when it suited her, "you aren't supposed to approve of this interest Simon has in me."

"Piffle. I'll keep the next couple in the roles of Katie and Simon apart. This is only a trial run. I can experiment if I want to." She took the bowl from Nessa's lap and the peeling knife from her hand. "Why don't you go find him right now? You know you want to. If it will help, you can pretend you *are* Katie. Surely *she'd* want to spend some time with Simon."

Grant was just coming down the outside stairs from his room in the barn when Nessa accosted him. She had a determined gleam in her eyes, reminiscent of the time she'd taken him on about clothing.

"Walk with me down to the pond," he suggested. Away from prying ears. Out of the corner of his eye, he saw Craig Seton come out of the chicken coop and stop to stare after them. Grant hoped the other man would keep his distance. He'd had enough of the fellow's griping for one day.

"Do country sounds bother you?" he asked Nessa, remembering Seton's most vocal complaint. "Keep you awake at night?"

"Not at all. Peepers make a nice change from traffic noise." She chuckled. "I think there may be a cricket in my bedroom. That's supposed to be good luck, isn't it?"

"Sure it's a cricket?" Though the dry, sunny weather of the past few days had solidified things, the ground still had muddy patches. Grant took Nessa's elbow to guide her. She didn't shake him off.

"What else could be in the house?" she asked.

"Mice."

"Mice don't chirp. Craig says he thinks you have them in the barn, though. Maybe you need to get a cat."

"Snakes will take care of the mice," Grant said, more to see if he could get a rise out of her than because he thought they had reptiles in the barn. She responded with a grimace and a shudder.

So, the lady didn't like snakes. It was the first time he'd managed to surprise revulsion out of her. She'd met all his other challenges with an admirable equanimity.

Adaptable. That was the word for her. Unless she had a good reason to object to something. Then she fought tooth and nail for her position and compromised only as a last resort. That strength of character aroused his curiosity. He still knew very little about her.

As they strolled past the last outbuildings, the sun was low in the west but had managed to warm both earth and air and now beat down upon their heads as well. They had perhaps another hour of daylight left.

The stock pond the Westbrooks had created

by building a small dam beckoned to Grant, offering a place to be alone with Nessa. Just to talk, he assured himself. They'd agreed to be friends, hadn't they?

"You *sure* you like being out here in the boonies?" he asked. "With the snakes and all?" *Friends* were allowed to kid around with each other.

"Don't confuse me with my assistant," Nessa warned. "We rarely see anything the same way."

"Why keep him around, then?"

"He's good at his job."

"You seem to be managing the taping pretty well on your own."

Nessa stopped to watch two birds swoop low across the field ahead. "Why do you sound so surprised?"

"Because Seton told Hank you couldn't do the job without him. That's how he managed to worm his way in here."

"You don't like Craig much, do you?"

"Did you plan to have him here all along?" It annoyed him that she seemed to calmly accept the news that Seton had lied about her. Maybe it didn't matter to her. Maybe she had other reasons for wanting his company.

"Let me see if I have this right," she said, responding to the irritation in his voice with a testy note in her own. "You get to have an assistant but I don't—is that it?"

"That's not what concerns me. And you're

evading my question." Did that mean there *was* more between the two of them than business? "Seton admits he has no interest in history. He doesn't even have the benefit of the background information you received prior to coming here. This trial run is important, Nessa. Why is he here, assuming you didn't invite him because you need his help with the taping?"

"I do not need anyone's help." She was toying with that curl again, the same one she'd mangled on her first day there, when they'd met in the barn.

He wished he hadn't remembered that particular moment. He'd almost kissed her a short time later. If Mary Ellen and Jason hadn't arrived—

And here he was walking with her, enjoying her company even when she continued to defend her worthless coworker.

They'd reached the small pond. Beyond, a rocky hillside rose up, catching the sunlight. "There's something the Westbrooks called the Indian cave up there," he said, deciding it was time to move on to a less controversial subject. "We may be able to run an archaeological dig one of these days."

Nessa shifted gears herself with admirable ease. She also asked knowledgeable questions, revealing her awareness of what tribes had once inhabited the area. He wasn't surprised when she admitted the information had come from another one of the segments on her show.

"We profiled the Lenni-Lenape," she told him, "since at one time they populated areas of New York, New Jersey, Pennsylvania, and Delaware."

"You seem to do as many stories on historical themes as you do on social issues."

"I like history," she said simply.

Together they inspected the two buildings near the pond, an old icehouse in need of repair and a boathouse. A small rowboat was tied up at the dock, the oars in it.

"You know this was a working farm," Grant said. "The Westbrooks supplemented their income by taking in summer boarders and in the winter they ran an ice business."

"I did not invite Craig here," Nessa said, putting a stop to his incipient lecture. "He decided on his own to join the party."

Grant wanted to believe her, but he couldn't help feeling there was something she wasn't telling him. "Are you involved with him?"

"He's my assistant on the show. Nothing more."

"He gives a different impression."

"Do you always accept appearance as truth?"

He winced. That shot hit a little too close to home. "The interviewer at work," he muttered, and stared into the pond's murky depths. Had it been a mistake to come out here with her?

"Do you have something against interviewers?" Her voice was so low and sultry that he needed to make a concentrated effort not to reach out and touch her.

"I have something against reporters," he admitted, "especially those on TV."

As soon as the words were out, he wished he could call them back. He didn't want to dredge up that whole mess. But if the look on Nessa's face was anything to go by, he was going to have to say something to clarify what he'd already revealed. He picked up a pebble and skimmed it across the water's surface.

"I think we need to clear the air," she said after a moment. "You've seemed suspicious of me, of my motives, from the first, and I don't believe I've given you cause to mistrust me. I shouldn't have to take the blame for what some other representative of the media did. Or if I must, then at least tell me what that person did to you."

"Old news." He tried to sound as if none of it mattered anymore. He knew better. Feeling the need for physical activity, he stepped out onto the dock. "Come for a ride with me?"

She hesitated, warily eyeing both dock and rowboat. "That thing better be sturdy. I'd hate to have to swim in this." She indicated all the layers of material she wore. Wet, they would weigh her down like a stone.

"I've tested this boat myself." To prove it he got in, then grinned up at her. "I swear I'll rescue you if you end up in the water."

Still looking skeptical, she lifted the bulky skirt

and its petticoats and joined him. It took some fancy maneuvering to lower herself and all that fabric onto the narrow seat, but she managed. In spite of her earlier objections to such outfits, she handled them as if she'd worn nineteenth-century clothes all her life.

Grant cast off and began to row. The rhythmic exercise relaxed him and for a little while his companion kept silent, apparently enjoying the solitude as much as he was. At first the only sounds on the water came from the steady dip and creak of the oars. Then a frog chorus began on the far shore.

"You were going to tell me about your bad experience with women and the media," Nessa said. "Or was it a woman in the media?"

"No, I don't believe I was. That subject is closed." It never should have been opened.

"I can find out on my own," she reminded him. "If you prefer, I can send Craig to Sidwell. Tell him we're going to do an investigative piece."

"Blackmail?"

"Just living down to your expectations, Professor."

She was teasing him again. Relief warred with chagrin. "You're not in a good position to make threats," he pointed out. "I might take you seriously and then I'd have to toss you overboard."

"Ah, but you already promised to rescue me if I was in the water, and I know you're a man of your word."

He stopped rowing, letting the boat drift as he leaned on the oars. "Six years ago," he said, "I was involved in a research project with a partner. A woman. I was also planning to marry her."

Nessa watched him now, her gaze steady as she waited for him to continue at his own speed. The interviewer at work, he mused, and yet, behind her calm exterior, he sensed there was something more. Her hands were tightly clasped in her lap.

"We disagreed on the results of our findings," he continued. "I wanted to check more sources. She felt we were ready to publish. While I was out of the country, trying to track down additional proof of our theory, she took everything we'd developed together and submitted it under her name alone. By the time I returned, it was already in print."

"I can see how that would sour you on women, but not on the media."

"A second woman had a hand in almost ruining my career. Since Corinne stole my work and published it as her own, I went public with charges of plagiarism against her. That's when she screamed sexual harassment."

"And the local press got hold of the story." Sympathy shone in Nessa's eyes.

"Oh, yes. Particularly one female reporter who decided to make an example of me. Her stories blew everything out of proportion."

"Did the case go to trial?"

He nodded. "And I won, a fact that was reported with a short item in small print on page ten of the local newspaper. On TV the story of the verdict never ran. No retraction was ever offered for certain statements made on the air. I suppose that reporter is still convinced I was guilty." And Grant was still smarting from his experience, even though working the last five years on the Westbrook Farm project had helped him put things into perspective.

"You didn't go on to sue the TV station, I take it."

"I'd had my fill of lawsuits and lawyers by then."

"I can sympathize with that," she said feelingly, making him wonder what experience she might have had, and on which end of a lawsuit. Before he could ask, she started talking again. "Journalism is supposed to be unbiased. Not all reporters are like that one you encountered. I know. I was one myself for a time, before I started the morning show."

A knee-jerk reaction had him speaking before he could censor himself. "Wonderful," he said, starting to row again. "Hank invited the paparazzi into our midst."

Nessa's eyes widened. Her mouth opened with a sound of protest. Grant would have apologized, but before he could get a word out, she grabbed one of the oars as it started its ascent and held on. Startled, he just stared at her, bereft of speech.

"I'm not either of those women," she said through gritted teeth. "You can't blame me for what they did."

Her intensity made the wood beneath his hand vibrate. Droplets of water fell from the end of the oar into the pond, extraordinarily loud in the charged silence.

"I'm sorry. You're right," he said. But he did find it difficult to trust her because of his experience with Corinne and that reporter.

With obvious effort, Nessa released the oar. Grant resumed rowing. In spite of the gathering twilight, he could make out the unhappy expression on her face, but he couldn't begin to guess the nature of her thoughts.

After a few moments, she spoke. "Thank you for telling me your story. Knowing what happened does help clear the air."

He cleared his throat. "While we're clearing things up, I have another question."

"About Craig," she guessed.

"If you didn't invite him and he knows you don't need his help, why did he come here? What does he want?"

"Let's call it misguided loyalty." She trailed her fingers in the water, watching the patterns she made rather than look at him.

"Explain."

"He believes taking a vacation just now was a major mistake on my part. Especially since I refused to leave a phone number where I could be reached."

"And why would anyone need to contact you? You're not married, right? No kids? You've never mentioned having a sick mother or a house full of pets."

With a sigh, Nessa wiped her wet fingers on the green skirt and met his eyes. "There's a possibility of a syndication deal for my show. Craig is convinced the call will come in this week and that a decision will have to be made immediately if we don't want to blow it."

Her flat recital of the facts gave no indication of how she felt about the prospect. That puzzled him. Going for a national spot seemed a logical next step for a local talk show host. "Why didn't you just turn me down?" he asked. "Stay put and wait for the call?"

"You offered me a chance at something I've wanted to do for a long time. This syndication thing . . . Well, let's just say I'm not as convinced as Craig is that it's a step in the right direction."

"Does Hank Gilbert have anything to do with your being here? On a personal level, I mean."

"Do you think every man I meet wants a personal relationship with me?" She seemed surprised by that concept. He didn't know why she should be. She must know she was beautiful.

"Just answer my question, will you please?"

"I met Hank for the first time when he arrived

with Craig, but he found out about my interest in making documentaries through a mutual friend. A woman named Taffy Kopatnic."

Meaning Hank was romantically involved with Nessa's friend, not Nessa. He shouldn't feel such a sense of relief, Grant told himself. The only thing he should care about was that nothing interfere with the program he'd set up for this week. He should simply ignore the personal lives of the people gathered there. Volunteers, that's all they were. At the end of the week, everyone but Bea and Doug would go his or her separate way. He'd start interviewing people for the remaining permanent staff. Vanessa Dare would go back home and edit the documentary.

But in spite of all his good intentions, his firm resolutions, he found himself once more focusing on her mouth. He couldn't remember when he'd wanted to taste a woman's lips more than he did at that moment—except for the last time he'd been alone with Nessa.

He couldn't seem to get a handle on his responses to her, let alone put a stop to them. He wanted to reach across the rowboat and hold her, breathe in the scent of her soap and the more elusive aroma that was hers alone. His whole body tensed as desire rippled through it. He fought the instinct urging him to take her into his arms. This was an absurd situation he'd gotten them into. And this wasn't a woman he should pursue, chemistry or not.

Steeling himself against the inevitable, impending sense of loss, he turned the boat toward the nearest shore. The best thing he could do was get them back to the house fast. There were plenty of chaperons there. She'd be safe from him. He'd be safe from himself.

SEVEN

By the time the boat touched ground by the dam, Nessa seemed as anxious to go ashore as he was. Without waiting for him to assist her, she clambered out, nearly tripping over her skirts in the process. She took two steps on the soft earth, tottered, let out a shriek, and froze.

"What? What's the matter?"

She was staring in horror at the low water near the dam. "I think I just stepped on a snake. A big one."

There was no sign of anything more threatening than a stick lying on the muddy ground. He thought it likely she'd slipped on that, or maybe trod on a root concealed by the slime. It was too early in the year for snakes. "Did it bite you?" he asked as he got out of the boat, just in case he was mistaken. If she'd been bitten, she'd know it.

"No." She had gone dead white and her lips

trembled. "I'm not sure where it is. Or what kind it was." She seemed certain there had been a snake. He was equally sure her imagination had run away with her. They had been talking about snakes earlier. He'd led her to believe there were some inhabiting the barn.

His gaze on her quivering lips, he put his hands on her shoulders. She was trembling all over. She needed him to take care of her. To comfort her.

Grant's body hardened in a rush. He wanted to kiss her again more than he wanted his next breath.

"You're holding me too tightly," she whispered.

Abruptly dropping his hands to his sides, he fought to get himself under control. He was forgetting his own resolution to return quickly to the house, before anything more happened between them.

Cold-bloodedly, he set out to scare her away, exaggerating for effect. "Two varieties of snake are common in these parts," he said in his lecturing voice. "Milk snakes are big, but they're nonpoisonous. Then there are water moccasins. We're right at the northernmost edge of their territory. One of Katie's brothers was bitten on the arm by a water moccasin when he was a kid. It swelled up bad enough that he had to go to the doctor. He killed the snake first, though. Hung it up for everyone to see."

"Lovely." She just stood there, shaking harder. She ought to be running for the house. Didn't she know how dangerous it was to stay put?

Desperation made Grant creative. "In Tunis's daybook, he writes of the time Katie found a water moccasin in one of the sheds. It was going after baby swallows in a nest and that made her so mad, she forgot she was afraid of snakes and—"

Nessa clapped one hand over his mouth. "I don't want details! And the last thing I need is another lecture."

They were standing very close. Too close. The day's dying light aureoled her hair, mesmerizing him. He couldn't seem to help himself. As her fingers slid away from his lips to caress the nape of his neck, he slipped one arm around to the small of her back and the other into that enticing mop of red-brown curls, dislodging her cap, sinking his fingers into the soft, springy tresses.

"What *do* you need?" he murmured.

All his good intentions forgotten, he covered her mouth with his.

I need this, Nessa thought. *And more.*

For a few delicious moments, she gave herself over to enjoyment, savoring the feel of his lips on hers, his hands on her body and in her hair. Then she pulled free. Although she was careful where she stepped, she had more on her mind than snakes.

"Why now?" she asked in a whisper. "Why you?"

Smiling wryly, he bent to retrieve her cap and hand it back to her. He was careful not to brush her fingers with his in the process. "I'd be insulted by that question," he told her, "if I didn't think I knew exactly what you meant by it."

"This is—" She reached for the right word and could do no better than "—inconvenient."

"Love often is."

She felt her eyes widen and suspected her face had just drained of color too. "This isn't love. Not even close."

"Sure of that, are you?" His tone was mocking and his expression enigmatic. Even his eyes were shuttered, keeping her from divining his true feelings.

Irritated, she snapped at him. "Don't be absurd! Lust, sure. Sexual attraction." *Big time*, she added to herself. "But no more than that. It can't be."

"Interferes with syndication plans? Can't take any excess baggage along to La-La Land?"

Where had that come from? she wondered. Surely he didn't mean to suggest he was hurt because he'd fallen for her and thought she'd be leaving. Emotions that strong couldn't develop overnight. Could they?

She made no attempt to explain her real career goals. What she meant to do was irrelevant. Tempting as it was to picture Grant in her life after she left Westbrook Farm, that seemed highly unlikely.

He looked away from her, raking agitated fingers through his hair and destroying any semblance of neatness in the thick, coffee-colored locks. "Kissing you appears to scramble my brain," he said. "I say things I have no business saying."

She touched his arm, instantly sympathetic. "Kissing you has the same effect on me. Maybe . . . I guess we'd be better off if it doesn't happen again."

"You don't sound sure of that."

"I'm not," she admitted. She'd never felt like this before. Confused. Frustrated. Energized. Aroused. But one of them needed to be strong, for both their sakes. One of them needed to walk away.

Three hours later, Nessa was still wondering if she'd done the right thing. She tried to keep busy, to get her mind off Grant. It wasn't easy when they were living in the same house, practically in each other's pockets. Except for the brief periods when he was elsewhere, like right now when he was checking on the animals, there was rarely more than the length of a room between them.

Since shooting nighttime scenes was possible with the battery-powered lights attached to her camera, Nessa kept taping that evening, but no amount of work could entirely occupy her mind. It kept drifting to the man at the center of all this, to the not-so-stuffy professor she'd begun to think of in a whole new way, especially after his revelations during their boat ride. About what had happened after . . . Well, that had to have been a mistake even if it had felt so right.

Don't dwell on that now, she warned herself. Speculation was counterproductive. If anything, she should remember what he'd told her about the faithless Corinne and the nameless TV reporter and take that as evidence he couldn't be interested in her, not for more than a brief fling anyway.

She didn't do flings. She wasn't even particularly good at long-term love affairs. Those in her past had been few and far between. Always before, her career had been far more important than any relationship. Compromise for the sake of keeping a man had been an anathema to her.

Although she still appeared to be watching the others, who were attempting to make ice cream in an authentic White Mountain Freezer, Nessa lowered her camera. Her mind strayed from the documentary to contemplate how hollow her career had become and how alive she felt when she was with Grant.

When he returned to the kitchen, she was at once aware of him. Her head swiveled his way in time to intercept a glance that seemed filled with longing . . . and with regret.

A shout of laughter brought her back to what

she was supposed to be doing. She shouldered the camera once more, but she could not still the sudden racing of her heart.

"Jeez, this is hard work," Craig complained, rubbing the arm he'd worn out turning the crank. Mary Ellen took over. Nessa kept taping.

"I thought you wanted to show a man doing domestic chores," Jason said. "Not that I'm volunteering."

"You already volunteered to eat the result," Nessa shot back. "I mean to hold you to that promise."

"Get Grant to crank."

"Mary Ellen is doing just fine. And impromptu changes in the taping sometimes end up being better than the most carefully planned shots." Besides, she didn't think she'd be wise to focus on Grant more than she was. Staring at him through a lens would be extremely disconcerting.

"There must be a trick to it," Mary Ellen muttered when her arm, too, gave out. There was still nothing recognizable as ice cream in the tub.

"Maybe we got the proportions on the ingredients wrong," Bea suggested. "All we have to go on is a very vague recipe." She held a handwritten cookbook that had belonged to Ella Westbrook. It tended toward the "pinch" of this and "handful" of that school of measuring.

"Is it edible?" Nessa asked. She looked pointedly at Jason.

Her subjects cooperated, but not without making a great many faces and several rude comments. Just as she had the perfect shot lined up, her lightbar flickered and died. The camera stopped dead too.

"Oh, great," she muttered. "Just a second. Hold that pose. I have to change the battery pack."

"Need help?" Grant asked, appearing at her side.

"This happens all the time. Usually just at the moment when a once-in-a-lifetime, award-winning event is taking place." Her fingers shook a little as she worked. Grant was standing too close. And not nearly close enough. Uncomfortably aware of him, and of Craig watching them, Nessa started to babble. Anything to fill the tense, volatile silence. With the wry thought that his tendency to lecture probably stemmed from a similar impulse, she told him about a fund-raiser her TV station had sponsored the previous summer.

"So I agreed to be in the dunking booth," she went on, "for one shot for the camera. Time after time the ball missed. Then, the one time it hit, the camera's battery failed. I dried off and agreed to do it again. And another battery failed. It took three dunkings before we finally got that shot and let me tell you, that water was cold!"

"Ever think it might have been deliberate on the cameraman's part?"

"Not till now."

"Seems like it would be easy to sabotage, just for the pleasure of seeing you in a wet T-shirt." He looked as if he'd surprised himself with his words, which was oddly endearing.

"I'm sure it was just dumb luck. It doesn't seem to matter if the batteries that keep a field camera running are fresh or on their last legs when we start, they can last anywhere from twenty minutes to two days."

"Something like the gremlins who take up residence in a computer and deliver random lines of gibberish?"

"Exactly."

They smiled at each other. For a moment, Nessa forgot there were other people in the room and got lost in the dark depths of Grant's luminous eyes. He made no attempt to move toward her, but she felt his nearness in every fiber of her being. Her body ached to lean closer, to touch.

A loud throat-clearing noise brought her back to her senses. Craig was glowering at them, Mary Ellen seemed unsettled, while the others merely looked amused.

Nessa drew in a deep, steadying breath. "Go away," she muttered to Grant. "I'm trying to work." In a louder voice, she addressed the entire group. "Okay, let's try this again."

Thirty minutes later, when the new battery let her down, Nessa took it as a sign to give up for the night.

❖———————❖

The next morning after breakfast, Nessa announced she had to go into town because *all* her batteries were dead. "I need a few hours at an electrical source to recharge them," she explained.

Bea immediately came up with a list of supplies she could use, and Craig cornered Nessa. To Grant's eyes, they seemed to be quarreling. He moved closer, his protective instincts aroused. He was feeling strangely possessive too.

"Come on," Seton was wheedling. "You know you want company. And I can help you find a place to recharge. How about a motel room?"

"I have to pick up some things in Strongtown," Grant cut in. He was just being practical, he told himself. This had nothing to do with Seton or the possibility that he might persuade Nessa into anything. "There are outlets at Sidwell you can use."

Was it his imagination, or did Nessa seem relieved by his offer? "Excellent," she said.

Seton's reaction was also easy to read. Dislike. Mistrust. As Grant left the two of them, his acute hearing picked up a whispered warning.

"I'm a big girl, Craig," Nessa answered. "I can take care of myself."

"You barely know the guy."

Grant didn't wait around to hear Nessa's reply to that. He changed into jeans and a long-sleeved shirt and met Nessa at the van, then drove directly to the campus. The trip took less than an hour over a series of back roads. He knew the route well enough to have driven it in his sleep.

Upon entering his office, Nessa stopped short at the sight of the computer on his desk. "Twentieth century? Do my eyes deceive me?"

He ignored the sarcasm and went to check the mail that had accumulated in his absence while she busied herself with her batteries. When they were all plugged in and merrily recharging, however, she gave his office a more protracted survey.

"VCR. TV. Computer. Tsk, tsk, Professor. You've been hiding your true nature."

"I use modern gadgets in my real life all the time." He tried to sound repressive. He failed. Her teasing got to him, engendering the desire to answer back in kind. "There's another computer at my apartment, and I know you'll find this astonishing, but I even have indoor plumbing there."

"Wow. I'm impressed." Her smile was like a rainbow after a thunderstorm.

"We've got a couple of hours to kill," he said. "How about a quick tour of the campus."

The place was quiet, enjoyable to stroll around since most of the students were gone for spring break. He thought about suggesting they visit "the puddle," a small artificial lake in the middle of a quadrangle formed by four buildings, then thought better of it. Ponds were dangerous ground.

"This is charming." Nessa sounded like she meant it.

"Like Westbrook Farm, Sidwell College is a nice place to visit, but most people don't want to live here."

He really believed that, Nessa thought, but she would. Sidwell College was a typical small, red-brick-buildings kind of place, pretty and comfortable. She envied the folks who could call it home.

Like Grant.

A quick sideways glance told her he was keeping his distance, but they seemed able to walk in companionable silence. Maybe he was getting used to being around her.

Before she could contemplate that thought further, her stomach growled. Loudly. "It's noontime," she said, embarrassed.

"It doesn't take long to get used to those big dinners Bea fixes."

"Guess we'd better think about lunch."

"You like diners?"

"Sure. I also know they're rarer than hen's teeth these days."

"This one's been retrofitted," he told her. "And it also serves the best food in town."

He did not warn her about the decor, which surprised a delighted chuckle from her. The diner had been restored to resemble what it must have looked like in the fifties and sixties and even had a jukebox with oldies but goodies on it.

"I might have known you'd go for someplace

historical," she teased him as she slid into a vinyl booth and picked up the menu lying on the Formica tabletop.

Lunch was excellent, and they took turns making choices on the play selector at their table. There were no songs later than 1965. "Moon River" accompanied cups of corn chowder. "Leader of the Pack" provided background to sandwiches and chips.

"Dessert?" Grant asked.

She'd been studying the menu again. A giggle escaped her as she pointed to the selections under Homemade Ice Cream. "I've been wanting some since last night," she confided.

"Me too." The husky note in his voice startled her, and her laughter died at the look in his eyes. He'd taken his glasses off and set them on the table. There was nothing to shield her from the heat in his eyes.

"Ice cream," she said.

"That too." He signaled to the waitress to take their order.

Thank goodness the service was good, Nessa thought when two cones were delivered a few minutes later. A charged silence existed between them, one she did not know how to short-circuit. Cut the wrong wire, she thought wryly, and everything could blow up in her face.

Grant licked his cone first, a movement so slow and sensual that for a moment Nessa lost her train of thought. No man should be allowed to exude so much sex appeal just sitting in a diner eating ice cream.

With an effort, she focused her attention on her own cone. It was a vain hope that eating it would cool her down as long as she was staring at Grant. The man looked extraordinarily appetizing himself, and he made devouring maple-walnut in a sugar cone as erotic an act as she'd ever witnessed.

She caught a cold drop of her own burgundy-cherry ice cream as it dripped off the bottom of her waffle cone and saw his eyes follow the movement of her tongue. He looked . . . hungry.

Rattled, Nessa hastily bit into the crunchy rim. With her free hand she began wreaking havoc on a strand of her hair, then dropped the mangled lock when she realized what she was doing.

A tune someone else had selected came on the jukebox, country this time, a heartbreaking ballad of hopeless love. Nessa and Grant continued to watch each other eat. Grant slowly polished off the remainder of his ice cream, all the while regarding Nessa through lowered lids, a lazy look that made her think—

She shook her head to clear away the all-too-graphic images of the two of them making love. "Surely my batteries must be recharged by now," she blurted.

His smile gave her words a double meaning. She couldn't seem to get away from Freudian slips today. Nessa swallowed the last bit of her dessert and nervously wadded up her napkin. She had to get out of there. Now. Before she suggested doing something she'd *really* regret.

"Nessa." Her name on his lips stopped her in midflight. "Sit back down." She sat. She picked up her glass and took a sip of water, wishing it were something stronger. "Level with me, Nessa. Cards on the table, okay?"

She nodded.

"Are you as turned on as I am?"

"Yes." The word was only a whisper of sound, but he had no trouble hearing it. She stared deep into his dark eyes, searching for the spark she knew had to be there. She'd seen it before, the sexual hunger that matched her own. What they were contemplating wasn't the best kind of relationship to have, but she couldn't stand this wanting much longer.

He looked like he longed to kiss her again. And she needed him to. Stupid move or not, she wanted to make love with him. His eyes promised heaven.

"We need privacy," he said, "if we're going to continue this conversation. My apartment—"

She squeezed her eyes shut. "Yes." This time she spoke much too loudly. Heads turned. Grant lost no time paying for the meal and hustling her out to the van. "I'm not going to change my mind," she assured him as she got in.

She knew this was crazy. Craig had been right.

She didn't know all that much about Grant, but she had a feeling she was about to learn a great deal. Anticipation filled her as they peeled out of the parking lot. His blatant need for her thrilled her. She couldn't specify what it was about him that affected her so strongly, but she was sure of one thing. She wanted to find out where the pull between them could lead.

He drove directly to his place, a second-floor apartment not far from campus. He barely gave her time to glance around before he started kissing her. "Forget the decor," he murmured, but she had time to see that he had an extraordinary number of framed maps on his walls. Old maps. Including one that showed the location of Westbrook Farm in 1875.

He dropped a kiss on the side of her neck. Encouraged when she hummed with pleasure and relaxed against him, he nibbled on her ear. With excruciating slowness, he worked his way around to her mouth, sipping at her lips before he stroked his tongue across the lower one. She opened for him, snuggling closer.

Grant did not have to be asked twice. He took the kiss deeper, molding her against his body with one hand at the small of her back as the other swept down to caress the curve of her hips. When it came up again, it took her sweater with it, off over her head.

He released her mouth only to kiss his way to her jaw and across her ear to the back of her neck, turning her as he went. As he planted light kisses along her spine, Nessa shuddered with pleasure.

Still behind her, he reached around her to lower the zipper on her slacks and tug them over her hips. He kept kissing his way down her back until he stopped at the top of her French-cut bikini panties. "That's the most erotic thing I've seen in years," he murmured.

"What?"

"You have dimples. One on each side." He touched two spots on the rounded flesh just where the lace began, and then, apparently unable to stop himself, bent to kiss each one. When he paused to lave each with his tongue, Nessa's knees nearly buckled.

Any last-minute reservations vanished when he scooped her up into his arms and carried her toward his bedroom. Her surroundings whirled around her, forcing her to cling to him to steady herself. By the time she'd caught her breath, he'd lowered her onto his bed and was throwing off his clothes. His shirt went one way, his shoes another. Nessa shimmied out of her underwear as he undid his belt and jerked down his zipper.

Grant froze, eyes fixed on her bared body. She stared back, riveted by what was revealed in the gradually widening V at the opening in his jeans. Slowly, she levered herself upright, then rolled onto her knees. He didn't move as she edged toward him, not until she placed her hands on his waist.

Working together, they divested him of his remaining clothing, until the extent of his desire for her was fully revealed.

With a muted groan, he embraced her, and the same movement sent them both sprawling onto the bed. His weight atop her was delicious, the feel of him exactly what she'd been craving. Nessa shivered with delight as he drew his palm down over her stomach, then caressed lower.

"Grant," she murmured, lifting herself against him.

He needed no further invitation, but stroked and pleasured her as she did the same for him.

"I want you inside me," she whispered. She ached for him, and was surprised to discover just how much she did want him. She had never felt such urgency with anyone else.

"Soon," he promised, as his fingers probed gently, building her excitement, heightening her anticipation.

She didn't want to wait, not this first time. Parting her thighs, she reached out to capture him as intimately as he held her. He was hot and heavy in her hand, throbbing with his own need.

Voice raspy, he warned her to wait while he donned protection. She resented the delay, even though she appreciated his care for her, but in a moment he was back, poised at the entrance to her body.

For an instant there was resistance as muscles unused to the activity tightened and sought to deny him entrance. Grant pushed slowly forward, then withdrew.

Nessa's eyes flew open, her hips lifting to call him back, a word of protest slipping past her lips before she recognized the look on his face. He had no intention of stopping, but he did seem inordinately pleased to find this small indication that he was the first man she'd taken to bed in a long, long time.

"Easy, baby," he crooned. "No need to rush." He repeated the movement, the slow advance, the frustrating withdrawal. Left to his own devices, he'd keep on making those shallow thrusts, torturing her.

She was not in the mood for any more sensual teasing. Her hands, which had been clutching the bedspread beneath her, settled on each side of his head and dragged his face down to hers. "I need you now," she said, and fastened her lips on his.

She felt him smile in the moment before he obliged her, slowly driving himself into her as her body stretched to accommodate him.

The fullness within her was all she'd hoped for. As she felt her inner muscles close around him and cling, she slid her hands down the taut muscles in his back and brought her legs up to wrap around his lean hips. When her heels brushed across his backside, she felt him shudder.

Locked together, they paused, but only for an instant. Then they were both caught up in the ancient, pounding rhythms of lovemaking. There was nothing scholarly or pedantic about the way Grant Bradley made love. He did try at first to maintain control, withdrawing almost all the way and then thrusting fully into her, but when he attempted to repeat the motion, intent on giving her maximum pleasure, she trapped him inside her with answering movements of her own, forcing him to her will. With each stroke, he was less in command, and she reveled in his surrender. It didn't matter that she was soon flying out of control as well. Only that they be together in the final culmination.

"Now," he gasped.

"Yes," she whispered.

And as one, they climaxed, an explosion of pure sensation before blissful oblivion consumed them both.

EIGHT

A long time later, Nessa opened her eyes to find Grant watching her. She reached up to rearrange a lock of hair that had fallen across his brow and let her fingers linger to caress his ear, his nape. A contented sigh escaped her.

"Yeah," he agreed, and bent to drop a kiss on her lips. As he lifted his head, his gaze fell on her bare shoulder. He brushed across the bruises there with his fingertips. "Camera?"

She nodded. "The price of perfection."

"I can't help but admire a perfectionist," he murmured, but when she reached out to draw him close again, he moved away. He was getting up. Getting dressed. Leaving her.

"I don't have anyone waiting for me," she whispered, stretching and settling herself against the pillows once more.

"We need to get back. The others are expecting us by suppertime. They'll be worried if we're late."

She tried not to let her disappointment show as she swung her legs over the side of the bed and sat up. It was obvious she hadn't succeeded when she felt his weight drop down beside her. Edging close, he slipped an arm around her shoulders. "I'm just trying to be practical, Nessa. There's no sense advertising that things between us have changed."

"And when we're back at Westbrook Farm? Do we . . . continue?"

He looked away. "I don't know."

Standing up, Nessa began to dress. This wasn't working out quite the way she'd expected. She didn't want to leave. She wanted to stay right there, possibly forever. The old "can't get enough" sex syndrome had kicked in with a vengeance. Not entirely unexpected, but not particularly welcome, either.

"This was a mistake," she said.

"Maybe."

"No maybe about it."

But as they silently gathered their belongings, then went to pick up Nessa's batteries and begin the journey back into another century, she had the uneasy feeling that they were likely to make exactly the same mistake again, just as soon as an opportunity arose.

❖————————❖

He was gazing at her like a moonstruck calf.

The realization almost made Grant laugh. He *would* have laughed if he hadn't been so appalled by his own behavior. He'd spent most of the previous night alternately regretting and relishing the fact that he'd made love with Vanessa Dare. Obviously the theory that, once having had a woman, a man could get her out of his system, was pure malarkey.

That morning Nessa was up in an apple tree with her camera, looking for the best angle for a long-distance shot of the pond. She hadn't been close to it since the incident with the snake. Or root. Or stick. Or maybe she'd finally figured out *he* was the snake.

When she came down, she stopped to wash her hands at the now-functioning watering trough. The wooden sluiceway he'd constructed brought a steady stream of water from the spring, which made the trough much easier to use than the pitchers and basins in the rooms. She took her time, giving her forearms and face a good splash while she was at it. He understood now that it was backbreaking, mind-numbing work to put a documentary on video.

She looked up and caught him staring. "I don't suppose you'd reconsider Doug's notion of rigging up a shower? They must have had them."

"Outdoors, maybe." He walked over to her, trying to quell the image of taking a shower with Nessa. Lathering her up with Ivory soap. He could smell the fresh, clean scent even before he reached her side.

"So? When are you going to build one?"

"The Westbrooks didn't have a shower."

"How do you *know* that? And don't tell me that it's because there's no record of building one in Tunis's daybooks. I expect there are lots of things he didn't record. Whether Nathan smoked, for instance."

"How often Tunis made love to his wife, for instance?"

Nessa's smile was shaky. "There's an image I do not want in my mind."

"Neither do I." Mary Ellen seconded Nessa's opinion, startling Grant when she spoke. He'd been concentrating so completely on one woman that he'd never even noticed the other's approach.

"I saw you up in the apple tree," Mary Ellen told Nessa. "Too bad spring is so late this year and they aren't flowering yet. If you could capture that moment of budding, it would symbolize the birth of the project."

Nessa seemed a bit taken aback by the idea of using imagery, but she smiled politely. Grant wondered if she was regretting Mary Ellen's arrival and the loss of their privacy as much as he was. His gaze locked on Nessa, Grant paid no attention to the younger woman until he heard her gasp in pain. He turned to find her clutching her middle. Then she bolted for the house.

"What the hell?"

"I'll go after her," Nessa said. "She must be ill."

An hour later, when Nessa went to check on Mary Ellen for the second time, she found Westbrook Farm's hired girl languishing in bed. At the sound of her door opening, Mary Ellen glanced up, lifting one limp hand to a wan cheek. When she saw it was only Nessa, disappointment flickered in her eyes. And something else. Irritation? Anger? Jealousy?

Although Mary Ellen's room was directly across a narrow hall from Nessa's, Nessa had never entered it before. She was surprised to see how much smaller Mary Ellen's quarters were than her own and struck by the stark simplicity of the "maid's room." The walls were unpapered and the windows had neither blinds nor curtains. Instead of a wardrobe, there was a rod in the corner on which to hang clothing. The best that could be said for the furniture was that it had a certain primitive charm. A single bed was flanked by a chest of drawers with a small mirror on top and a matching washstand, both made of pine. The only luxuries were a small rag rug on the wide-board floor and a flowered china washbasin.

"Is there anything I can do for you, Mary Ellen?" Nessa asked.

"Probably not. I'm feeling much better now. I must have eaten something that didn't agree with me." She'd obviously felt well enough to change into a rather sheer nightgown.

"Aren't you cold?"

A calculating look came into Mary Ellen's eyes. "Yes, I am. You know, it's probably much warmer on your side of the house, where the sun's been coming in through the windows all morning. Would you mind trading rooms with me? This should have been your room in the first place anyway."

That made perfect sense, since the front room Nessa had been sleeping in was the best in the house. Ella and Tunis had likely kept it for themselves during the off-season and rented it out as the most expensive room in the house during the summer. "Where did Molly sleep?"

"Probably in a corner of the kitchen. I'm sure they wouldn't have given her space in the barn. Too tempting for her to be that close to the hired hands."

"You don't seem tempted by Craig," Nessa observed.

"Not my type." Mary Ellen was looking healthier by the minute, and it occurred to Nessa that she had expected Grant to be sleeping alone in the barn. Or perhaps not so alone. Tottering slightly, Mary Ellen got out of bed and started toward the door. She was across the hall and installed in Nessa's bed before Nessa realized what she was up to. Carefully posed, too, Nessa mused, looking lovely and frail and in need of comforting.

"I need to see the professor," she told Nessa. "Will you be a darling and send him up?"

Promising to give Grant the message, Nessa slowly descended the stairs to the sitting room where the others waited. She didn't know quite what to tell them about Mary Ellen. She was beginning to suspect the other woman had faked her illness. But why? To capture Grant's attention? To shame Nessa into trading rooms? Or simply to get out of doing so much hard work? Malingering, they'd have called it in the old days.

"How is she?" Grant asked as soon as Nessa entered the room.

"She wants to talk to you."

"Find out what it's about, will you, Seton? If she's changed her mind and decided to go see a doctor, you can take her."

"She wants to talk to *you*," Nessa repeated. "And she's in my room."

"The rest of us have something important to discuss," he told her once Craig had left. He gestured toward the corner of the sitting room and for the first time Nessa realized Hank was back.

"Something you don't want Craig to hear?" she asked, taking a seat on the piano bench.

"He's not directly concerned. You are. Because of the documentary, you have a stake in the success of this project."

"A project now in jeopardy," Hank said.

"What! Why?"

"Mary Ellen's sudden illness opens up a potential problem for the living history center," Hank said, taking control of the discussion.

"That's why we're having this trial run, isn't it? To find flaws?" Jason sounded ingenuous, but Nessa thought she saw something more in his expression. Avarice? No, surely she was mistaken. She was assigning ulterior motives to everyone today.

"What problem?" she asked.

"Insurance. Safety issues again. What if a paying customer gets sick? If food poisoning is the cause, we could be sued. And what if Mary Ellen had had a hot appendix?"

"If someone gets sick, we transport that person to the nearest doctor, or to a hospital." Grant looked worried, but not overly so.

"And the lawsuit? We'll have to draw up some kind of release for everyone to sign. People don't like that sort of thing. Could be trouble."

"Oh, for heaven's sake," Nessa said. "Stop grandstanding, Mr. Lawyer. Folks don't hesitate to sign away their right to sue over injuries when they want to try bungee jumping. They aren't going to quibble over something with as few potential dangers as this has."

"Maybe they should," Jason said.

"Of course they *should*!" Nessa wasn't one to trust any document handed to her by a lawyer. "My point is that they don't."

"Safety issues concern me," Hank defended himself. "Westbrook Farm is out of touch with the rest of the world. Cut off. There could be all kinds of accidents in the barn. Some potentially fatal. A fall through the hay hole, for example."

"Or a snakebite," Nessa murmured.

Grant gave her a quelling look, but he spoke to Hank. "You're making a mountain out of a molehill, old buddy. Just write up an all-purpose waiver that includes accidental death and dismemberment as well as illness."

"The track leading from the parking area to the house is wide enough for an ambulance or a fire truck," Bea reminded them. "The only reason we walk up is because we don't want cars around to remind us what century this really is. From Luzon, an emergency vehicle can be at our door ten minutes after we call for it."

"Conditions here are not quite as primitive as you seem to believe, Hank," Grant added. "I've shown the others where all the smoke alarms and fire extinguishers are located. We have cellular phones. And locked up tightly in one of the sheds are a generator and industrial-strength extension cords and work lights."

"You're telling me I could have had a space heater in that ice-cold bathroom?" Craig had come back into the sitting room just in time to hear Grant's last statement.

"That wouldn't have been authentic," Nessa told him . . . before Grant could.

A space heater would have been nice in the bedrooms, too, Nessa thought some ten hours later. She lay awake staring at the ceiling, unable to settle down and sleep. This night was the mildest one yet, but she was in Mary Ellen's small room and neither the bed nor the blankets seemed as warm and snug as her own.

Moon and starlight streamed in through the uncurtained windows, another cause for wakefulness besides her continual, and deepening, confusion over Grant Bradley. She was suddenly seized by a desire to go outside. Maybe a bit of exercise would tire her enough to sleep.

A few minutes later, she was standing on the porch, breathing in fresh night air that carried the pleasant scent of freshly turned earth. Footsteps startled her, and she jumped when a dark shape advanced on her from the direction of the barn. She very nearly screamed and did assume one of the defensive positions she'd been taught by a martial arts expert who'd appeared on her show, ready to kick and claw her way to safety if it became necessary.

"It's only me."

"Grant?" She discerned his familiar silhouette in Simon's customary white shirt and loose trousers, and also saw that he was carrying some kind of bundle under one arm. "You could have been anyone," she said, straightening.

"Oh, yeah. We've got all kinds of murderers

and madmen running around in these woods. Shall I tell you the story of The Hook?"

"No need. You scared the socks off me already."

A more historically accurate expression would be "scared out of her drawers," but Grant refrained from verbalizing his errant thought. He did note that she appeared to be wearing a formfitting set of long johns as nightwear. An interesting choice.

"I'm sorry," he said aloud. "I didn't mean to frighten you."

"What are you doing out here?"

He quirked a brow at her, and she blushed. Or at least he assumed she did. The moon wasn't quite bright enough to tell. They were standing near the start of the path that led to the "necessary," next to one of several lilac bushes which in summer provided a covering scent. At night they cast spooky shadows.

"Not for that," he said. "I couldn't sleep in that room in the barn. Too stuffy. And Craig snores. I thought I'd camp out on top of that rock in the near field. Think about things." He pointed to the barely visible shape of a huge boulder in the middle of the meadow on the west side of the house.

"What things?" she asked.

You, he answered, but not out loud. Hoisting negligent shoulders, he spoke lightly. "Whatever comes to mind as I watch the stars." Before he could stop himself, he blurted out an invitation. "Would you care to join me?"

"It *is* a nice night," she said.

Neither one of them spoke again until they reached the rock and he showed Nessa where to put her feet to scramble to the top. He passed her his sleeping bag, then clambered up.

"All the comforts of home," she said when she'd spread the bag out and settled in at his side. The thick, insulated fabric counteracted both the hardness and the coldness of the stone beneath them.

"Lean back and you've got a great view of the constellations. You can't do this in town, not even on campus. Too many lights. I often camp out here when I'm working on repairs."

They lay side by side, staring up at the sky. Bad idea, he thought. He wanted to roll over, slide her beneath him, and make sweet love to her for the rest of the night. He remained rigidly still, hoping the urge would pass, knowing all too well it was only going to grow stronger.

"The only stars I can ever recognize are those in the Big Dipper," Nessa confessed.

"The Indians called that Seven Brothers," he said. "I'd tell you the entire legend, but you'd probably accuse me of lecturing again."

He was close enough to feel her silent laughter. It sent a shiver of another kind straight through him. "Yes, I would. And if it's the kind of legend where people get to be stars because they die tragically, I don't want to hear it."

"Is there any other kind?" he asked. Blanketed in near darkness, it was easy to talk to her, even with his body crying out for hers. "Cruelly parted lovers reunited. Whole families slain. Or eaten by bears." A new topic of conversation seemed called for. "Thank you," he said.

"For what?"

"Coming to the defense of the project. I can see it now in our advertising: Safer than bungee jumping."

"Hank was being a jerk."

"Is it Hank you dislike, or lawyers in general?" Her animosity had been too marked to miss.

"Bad experience."

"Recent?"

He felt rather than saw her shake her head. "Practically ancient. I was just a kid." She hesitated. He slid an arm around her shoulders, silently offering comfort and encouragement. "I grew up poor," she continued after a minute. "When I was little, we had a house. It was taken away under eminent domain. My mother went to a lawyer for help. Then another. And another. Each one claimed to be able to save our home. The only ones who came out ahead were the lawyers. In the end, all our savings were gone and so was the house. We ended up living in low-income inner-city housing until I graduated from high school. It was everything you're imagining.

Gangs. Drugs. Domestic violence. Cockroaches as big as rats. Rats as big as—"

"Don't." Grant couldn't stand to hear any more. He pulled her close, kissing her until she quieted, but she remained rigid in his arms. The only softness about her was in the fabric of her long johns.

She did not kiss him back. When she pushed against his chest, he let her go.

"I never talk about any of that stuff." She sounded shaken.

"Blame it on the moon."

She made a choked sound he decided was an attempt at a laugh. Nessa wasn't the crying type.

"You survived a rough childhood. That's something to be proud of."

"Luck," she said dismissively.

Determination, he thought, but he let her talk without interrupting again. She didn't tell him much, but every little bit he learned made him admire her more. She and two sisters had been raised by a loving mother. They'd been taught to "make do" and to get all the possible good out of everything they owned. Which was pitifully little, he surmised. He understood now why she knew how to darn. He'd be willing to bet she'd made most of her own clothes until she'd finally found a job where she could earn enough to buy what she needed.

"How did you manage college?" he asked.

"Full scholarship. And a part-time job."

"That's not the result of luck."

"Landing my first job after college was. Luck and a face that photographs well."

The job as a reporter, he remembered, and realized that her profession no longer disturbed him quite so much. This woman deserved every bit of the success she'd achieved.

"Enough about me," she said. "What about you? Did you do most of the rebuilding here yourself?"

"Pretty much. I wanted it to be right."

"But how did you know what to do? How to do it?"

"My father owns a construction business, and he believes everyone should have some basic building and repair skills. He made sure all of us learned, even the girls. Even the son who was a bookworm."

"Always liked history, huh?"

"Always." Just as she'd said she had.

"And those star legends?"

"I've been doing research on Indian lore. Legends are a part of it."

"I wonder if there's a segment for my show in the subject," she mused. Now that they'd moved away from the discussion of her childhood, she seemed more relaxed. Her head rested on his upper arm. One hand lay nestled against his rib cage.

"Is everything you see or hear a potential segment to you?" His teasing tone hid a serious interest in her answer.

"No more than everything you encounter is a research project," she shot back. "Tell me, Professor, what's your focus here? Mary Ellen and the others may find things to write about in the Westbrook family's papers, but I have a feeling that isn't what you're working on."

She was guessing, he decided. But guessing well. Strangely, her interest didn't bother him. Somewhere along the line he'd decided he could trust her. "I plan to investigate the people who lived here before the Westbrooks."

She clamped her hand on his arm and sat up enough to lean over him and stare down into his face. "The Indian cave on the hill. Do you think there's something to be found there? Artifacts?" Her voice bubbled with excitement.

"Let me guess, you always wanted to go on an archaeological dig?"

"I've already been on an archaeological dig. *Give.*"

He laughed, delighted with her, with himself. "The Indian cave, such as it is, is a bust. The name probably got attached to it decades after the last Indians were gone from the area, but they *were* here. Near the spring. What I'm particularly interested in is how the original inhabitants of this land reacted to the earliest white men. Which brings me to another legend. Have you ever heard of Tom Quick?"

"I've heard of Tom Swift." He sensed she was

smiling as she mentioned the fictional hero of that old boys' adventure series.

"Not the same. Look in the *Sullivan County Directory* for 1872-3. It's in the writing room on the top shelf of the bookcase. There's a section in it that will answer all your questions."

"You *could* just tell me."

"Then you'd accuse me of lecturing."

"Anyone ever tell you you're a frustrating man?"

"Frustrated," he corrected her softly.

Still leaning over him, she sighed. "I'm beginning to regret giving Mary Ellen that lovely big double bed."

"Just as well."

"Ever do it on a rock?"

Biting back a groan, Grant sat up. "We're in full view of the house, and the moon is bright." Besides, although his ever-practical father had also taught his son never to go anywhere without protection, that particular "emergency gear" had not been transferred to Simon's pockets.

"I'm using Mary Ellen's room tonight," Nessa whispered. "She can't see a thing from mine."

"And right below Mary Ellen's old room is the one Bea and Doug occupy. Do you want to take the chance that one of them will happen to get up, happen to look out the window? Sometimes Bea's arthritis bothers her and she has to walk around a bit. She might even wander outside."

Her second soft sigh almost had him willing to

risk it, but it meant she knew he was right. Before he could change his mind and ask her to stay, to spend the rest of the night wrapped with him in sweet torment in his sleeping bag, she'd slid down the face of the rock and slipped out of reach.

From the bottom, she looked up at him. "Thanks for sharing your stargazing perch."

"Anytime."

He watched her walk away with a deep sense of regret and an ache that wasn't likely to stop anytime soon. But what shook him most was the knowledge that he'd meant his invitation. Any time she wanted to spend together, doing anything, was fine with him. He was dangerously close to falling in love with a woman who was all wrong for him.

NINE

During dinner the next day, it started to rain. Hard. After an hour, when they should have been getting back to their various afternoon chores, Grant's volunteers gathered in the sitting room for a second cup of coffee. He had to admit he didn't particularly want to venture out into the storm himself. It was far more pleasant to sit sipping a hot beverage while he watched Vanessa Dare stand at a window and stare out at the rain.

She was in her working clothes again. He should have disapproved, but all he could think of was getting her out of that sweatshirt and snug jeans. And if he succeeded, he didn't believe he was going to be in any hurry to get her back into a dress.

Shifting uncomfortably on the plush-covered settee, he stared into his cup. Had she become an obsession? He didn't like that possibility one bit. It was . . . she was . . . distracting.

"It's odd," Nessa murmured, "but this weather makes the farm seem much more cut off from the rest of the world. Things must be really eerie here in winter."

"It's no wonder turn-of-the-century rural New York State produced so many independent, strong-minded people." Jason glanced at the portraits of Ella and Tunis as he spoke. "Had to be that way to survive."

"They had it easy," Doug said. "Imagine what it was like in the 1790s."

A bolt of lightning flashed nearby, and Nessa shivered. "I'll pass. It's spooky enough with this storm in the 1990s." She left her post at the window and went to sit in the wing chair, picking up some mending on her way. Grant had noticed that she liked to keep her hands busy even when she wasn't in character as Katie.

"Think we'll have flooding?" Seton sounded nervous.

Mary Ellen laughed. She seemed completely recovered, Grant thought, though she was behaving a bit oddly around Nessa. Her attitude toward Seton was one of disdain.

Indignant at being mocked, Seton defended himself. "Hey, I remember that journal entry from the first night here. They had some pretty good flooding around these parts a hundred years ago. What's to stop it happening again? There's still snow in the mountains, even if this is April. If the rain melts it too quickly into already-swollen rivers, they could overflow their banks."

"We're on a hill," Grant reminded him. "At worst, we'll be cut off from town until things dry out, but since we aren't going anywhere until Sunday, we probably won't even know about it until after the entry road is passable again." He seriously doubted it would be a problem. Once the rain stopped, the ground would dry out quickly.

"Hank was smart to leave when he did," Seton grumbled.

Grant grimaced. Hank had left early that morning, full of schemes. He'd already come up with the wording for guests to sign away their right to sue the project for injuries, damages, or death. Now he was enthusiastically pursuing two agendas, one to con insurance companies into covering them for any contingency at bargain rates, and another for founding a nonprofit corporation to raise money and maintain the property. Now that Hank had thought of that, he was saying they should have done it at the beginning.

Unsure how he felt about this development, Grant had begun to think he should have been more involved in the business aspect of his project. He knew Nessa's documentary would help them find investors, and he had to wonder if this nonprofit corporation had been Hank's plan all along. Grant's own thoughts had run more along the lines of getting funding from the National Trust for Historic Preservation, or maybe some Title III money to help develop their program of day trips for schoolchildren. Approval was already pending to have Westbrook Farm declared a National Historic Site by the U.S. National Park Service.

"What if it's still raining Sunday when we're ready to leave?" Seton couldn't seem to stop fussing about floods.

"Highly unlikely," Bea declared. "Of course, there was that one year when we had an April Fools' Day snowstorm *and* a May Day flood."

Grant admired Bea's patience. With every one of Seton's whining complaints, he grew more tempted to toss the fellow out into the storm and let him fend for himself.

"Did you know that the legendary blizzard of 1888 affected these parts, Craig?" Mary Ellen asked. "There are mentions of it in Tunis Westbrook's daybook."

Nessa folded a shirt and set it aside, having replaced a missing button, and picked up a handkerchief that needed hemming. "Aside from indoor chores," she asked, "what would the Westbrooks and their boarders do to pass the time on an afternoon like this? Read? Play cards?"

"Maybe," Grant said. "Or they might simply talk to each other. Conversation wasn't a lost art back then. And storytelling used to be a normal part of life before radio, television, and CD players took over." He forced a smile and launched into an account of the drowned towns of Cantre'r Gwaelod, sixteen villages inundated by floodwaters in sixth century Wales.

Nessa's heart gave an erratic little beat at Grant's effort to entertain them. His tendency to fall back on lecturing now seemed endearingly human to her. She wondered how she'd ever perceived him to be aloof and stuffy.

The rain continued. Another hour passed comfortably in the dry, snug sitting room, especially after Jason and Craig found a chessboard and started a game. Bea took over the mending. Doug played softly on the piano. Mary Ellen retired to her room, saying she still wasn't feeling a hundred percent and needed a nap.

She said it to Grant, who missed her hint. How the man remained oblivious amazed Nessa, but she was glad he did.

She had no right to feel that way, she reminded herself. She had no claim on him. But when he rose from the settee and announced that someone had to brave the downpour to check the animals, she offered to go with him. "Besides, I left one of my tote bags in the barn," she said truthfully.

"I can bring it back in with me," he offered.

"It's too involved for me to explain where I left it. I'll just come along. Besides, I can help with the milking."

He gave her a skeptical look, but agreed.

How hard could milking a cow be? Nessa wondered. Craig had managed to master it. She found out a few minutes later. As they had when he showed her how to prime the pump, Grant's arms shadowed hers, his strong hands guiding her fingers into the rhythm needed to coax a thin, warm stream of milk into the tin pail.

The process was oddly sensual. But then, everything she did with Grant seemed to border on the erotic. She was clearly losing her mind, Nessa thought. Maybe she should reconsider doing that show her producer had suggested . . . on sex addiction.

They didn't talk while the milking was being done. They didn't talk afterward, either. Nessa suddenly couldn't think of a single thing to say. She wanted action, not words.

Her blood sang in her veins, calling to Grant. But when he reached for her, a sudden wave of panic had her backing away. She wanted him too much, not just with her body, but with her heart and mind, and that scared her. "Maybe this was a bad idea," she whispered.

Grant's intense gaze never wavered from her face. "Get your tote bag, then, and we'll go back."

"Oh. Yes." That had merely been an excuse to follow him out to the barn and they both knew it, but she had left one of her totes in the loft. "I'll just be a minute," she said in a rush, and scrambled up the ladder.

She needed a little distance from Grant. She

knew she ought to stop and consider what she was getting into before she took their relationship any further.

"Find it?" he called up to her. Whatever he was thinking, his voice gave nothing away.

It was much darker in the loft than she'd expected. "Shoot," she muttered. "I can't see a thing."

"I'll bring the lantern." A moment later, Grant stood beside her holding the light. "When did you leave one of your bags behind? I thought you finished all the interior shots in the barn days ago."

"I've been using this loft as a thinking place," she explained. When they were open, the big doors through which hay was hoisted in from the outside gave a splendid view. The storm crashed against them now, and bursts of moist air seeped in through the cracks. Nessa shrugged. "Most of the time it's quiet and the hay makes a good cushion. Last time I was here I made notes on the sequences I wanted to shoot in the addition."

A stronger gust of wind eddied through the closed doors, tossing a lock of hair into Nessa's face. Coming up there had definitely been a mistake, she thought, though she didn't really regret making it. She found the sound and smell of the storm invigorating, and Grant's presence even more so. They were cut off, isolated by sheets of rain so dense, she would barely be able to see the house if she opened the hay doors. Impelled by an urge she didn't fully understand, she slid one back a few inches and let the tempest in.

The picture she made standing there in the lantern light, her hair whipped wildly by the wind, could have been a scene in a movie, Grant thought. And the next scene was going to be X-rated. When she knelt in the hay to search for her tote bag, she looked impossibly desirable. He took a step toward her, all his resolutions to back off shot to hell. If he didn't hold her, didn't kiss her soon, he was going to explode.

Another burst of wind caught a loose shutter and slammed it against the outside of the barn, startling them both. Nessa let out a squeak of alarm and flung herself backward, straight toward Grant. He caught her easily, though he nearly dropped the lantern. He did not let go again, not even when she laughed at her own foolishness and tried to break free.

"Grant?" She lifted her head to stare at him. In the flickering light, her eyes appeared to be a darker blue, but they were no less alluring. The tiny lines at their corners begged to be kissed.

He didn't need to say a word. Pressed this close together, both the expression on his face and the state of his body revealed the extent of his desire to her. When she breathed his name again, it was not a question.

As frantic as if they'd never made love before, they kissed and caressed, scattering clothing impatiently. He barely had the presence of mind to set the lantern in a safe spot. He had her down to bare skin and himself stripped to his nineteenth-century Skivvies before he remembered that he still didn't carry protection in Simon's pockets.

"This can't go any further," he whispered.

"I don't see how it can stop." She kissed him again, hard and hot and powerful enough that it almost burned away his deep-seated sense of responsibility. "I'm willing. You're willing." She ran one hand down his chest, then lower to brush over the erection making his underwear bulge. "Ready and willing."

"Nessa, Simon's never had his consciousness raised."

Involved in touching him and tasting the skin on his chest, she didn't comprehend what he meant. "This isn't about Simon and Katie, Grant," she said breathlessly. "This is you and me. Grant and Nessa."

"I don't have a condom," he said bluntly.

"I . . . don't . . . care." She kissed him between each word, making him want her more urgently still, even though he knew they had to stop.

His wallet was in his room, which could not be reached from this hayloft without going down the ladder and up again by a set of stairs. Talk about killing a mood! He tried to pull away, which was difficult when they were half lying, half kneeling in a great mound of hay. When he rolled, she came with him, adding her weight to his as he encountered a hard, lumpy object.

"Damned tote bag," he mumbled, reaching beneath them to shove it out of the way.

"Oh!" she gasped, and sat up, pulling away from him.

He did not want to let her go, but he didn't see that he had any choice. "I guess I ought to be grateful," he said ruefully.

"No," she said.

"Nessa, we have to stop. The risks—"

"No. We have protection. In my tote bag."

"You carry condoms in your tote bag?" He didn't know whether to be elated or appalled.

She smiled. A beautiful smile, he thought. Then she turned away to burrow in the big canvas bag. "I toss all kinds of things into my totes and hardly ever clean them out. And if we're in luck, this is the tote that—" She broke off with a cry of triumph.

The package she held aloft was not a brand familiar to him. The shape seemed . . . different too.

"There was this segment I taped last week for my show," she said, glowing. "The piece hasn't run yet, but it's called 'Whatever Happened to the Female Condom?' "

When the contents of the small packet tumbled out into her hand, Grant could actually feel his eyes widen. The thing looked like some sort of mutated jellyfish. "You've got to be kidding."

"What? It's just a little wider than a male condom. The length is the same." It had two flexible rings, one on either end of the sheath. "It's inserted somewhat the way a diaphragm is." She flashed him a smile that was both mischievous and wanton. "Want to help, er, install it?"

But Grant was frankly repulsed by the object she held. It was alien. Vaguely alarming. And on closer inspection, there being so much of it, it seemed likely to interfere with a couple's pleasure. "We're not using that . . . thing."

Her eyes narrowed and she straightened her shoulders, drawing his gaze to her naked breasts. Instantly, his desire for her rekindled. Unfortunately, she was pulling away, a stubborn tilt to her jaw and a defiant challenge in her tone. "What's wrong with trying something new? This is very practical, especially for women foolish enough to get involved with men who don't bother taking precautions."

"I'm not one of them," he reminded her.

"No, but I guess *Simon* was!"

Grant dragged his fingers through his hair, exasperated. He ought to be completely turned off by this conversation. He *was* getting irritated and so was she, but somehow that only made him want her more.

"You don't have a regular condom with you now." Her eyes flashed as she spoke. Heat washed over him. "I'm offering a viable alternative."

They were very close. He could feel her intensity as if her every heartbeat, every breath, were his own.

"Nessa, you're torturing a needy man."

"And you have a needy woman on your hands," she admitted. She melted against him and kissed him softly on the lips as she wound her arms around his neck. "What are you going to do about that, Grant?"

She was infinitely hard to resist. He knew what she wanted him to do and resisted. Then inspiration struck. He had a better way to ease their mutual craving.

"Trust me to take care of you, Nessa," he whispered. "Let me have that newfangled contraption."

She smiled at his choice of words and complied, but her pleased expression vanished when he tossed the condom aside. "What are you doing?"

"Relying on the tried and true."

That was the last coherent thing Nessa heard for some time. One of her last rational thoughts was that she did trust Grant to protect her. Then his hungry kisses distracted her from worrying about anything but how good his body felt pressed against her own.

He toppled her into a soft bed of scattered clothing and hay, then kissed his way from her lips down to her breasts and over her belly and straight to the place that needed his attention the most. With languid strokes of fingers and tongue he pleasured her beyond her most fevered imaginings, driving her with beautifully tortuous strokes toward a cataclysmic release.

Relentless, he drove her up, up, up, until she was over the edge and falling into a climax that shook every centimeter of her body. When she finally exploded beneath his ministrations, she was only dimly aware that she cried out his name as she arched up, shuddering with her release.

Exhausted, she lay back, waiting for her breathing to steady, for her heart to stop racing. She gave one final shiver as he slowly kissed his way back up to her chin. His strong, gentle hands brushed sweat-dampened hair away from her face, and he settled in beside her on their makeshift bed.

"Wow," she whispered. She knew she was wearing a huge, sappy smile. She couldn't help herself.

"Beautiful," he murmured.

Nessa frowned. He sounded complacent, and he looked perfectly content. But he'd given her everything and taken nothing for himself. When he'd said he meant to rely on the tried and true, she'd thought he meant to withdraw at the last second, but he'd never entered her at all. He hadn't shared in that spectacular release.

"Grant, you didn't . . ."

"Actually, I did." He looked a trifle embarrassed.

"Oh."

After a moment he murmured, "One of these days we'll have to make use of that fine old bed in your room."

She liked the way he assumed there would be a next time. Right at that moment, she refused to think about all the things that might keep them apart. Instead she reached up and brushed her hand over the hint of a five o'clock shadow on his chin.

"One of these days, you'll have to be brave and try something new."

He didn't look convinced. "There's a reason that thing didn't catch on. If I'm typical, then men don't like it. Even women must think it looks weird."

"Some people don't mind a good laugh in the bedroom," she said in a tart voice. "And *that thing* works. Surely that's important."

They lay there together, watching the rain, sexually replete, but a note of disharmony had come between them at his adamant refusal to experiment with this particular result of modern technology. Nessa found she couldn't let the subject drop.

"I meant what I said earlier," she told him. "It's a godsend for a woman who wants to be intimate with a man who won't use a regular condom. It gives the woman an alternative. A choice. Besides which, statistics gathered by the manufacturer indicate that—"

"Are you lecturing me?" The words were said

in a teasing tone, but Nessa was unable to respond in the same vein.

"Someone should." Did he want to live entirely in the past?

"Hey, lighten up," Grant whispered, nuzzling her ear. "Aren't you the one who was just now advocating the joys of laughter?"

She'd been thinking along the lines of mutual giggling as they tried to insert a female condom, then falling into each other's arms in a wonderful combination of laughter and passion.

She supposed there was no point in trying to force him into the twenty-first century. And he'd certainly been right that his tried-and-true method was very good indeed. She could feel a small smile curve the corners of her mouth.

"Agree to disagree, okay?" he suggested.

What choice did she have? "Okay."

But she could not quite shake the feeling that not seeing eye to eye on this matter was a sign of deeper differences of opinion to come. He couldn't have made it clearer to her if he'd said it right out—Grant Bradley did not trust women or the solutions they offered.

He did not trust her.

Nessa sighed and sat up, reaching for her rumpled garments. For a few minutes, she'd forgotten how many differences existed between them. Now she had to face facts. What they had was at best a brief vacation fling. Their careers didn't give them much in the way of common ground. They lived hundreds of miles apart. His outlook on life was separated from hers by hundreds of *years*.

"There's something powerful at work between us," he said softly. "It goes deeper than just good sex."

"Does it?" She slipped into her underwear.

"Logic goes right out the window when I'm with you." He caught her by the waist, trying to tug her back down beside him. "I want you again."

This time it was her turn to resist. "Forget it, Grant. You tossed away my only—"

"We could dress. Go to my room." His hand ran up her calf, setting off sparks. "Undress."

"Your room? You mean the one with the rope beds and the roommate who snores?"

He released her, stood, and began to throw on his clothes. She'd made him angry again, but this time it wouldn't lead to other passions.

Nessa stopped with the rest of her clothing crushed to her chest and stared at him as he dressed. The man was mouthwatering. She shook her head to clear it and stepped into her jeans. All that perfection and one gigantic flaw. "You hate to compromise, don't you?"

"I thought I came up with a pretty . . . satisfying compromise a little bit ago."

She jerked her gaze away from him and buttoned her blouse, then pulled her sweatshirt over her head. "I mean you won't try anything new," she muttered. "At least nothing new to your closed mind. You're stuck in the past, even when you're at the college or at your apartment."

He tucked his shirttail into his pants and stared at her in obvious bewilderment as he pulled up his braces. "For an intelligent woman, you sometimes make no sense at all."

"I'm making perfect sense. I can move from century to century. I'm even looking forward to the twenty-first! Can you say the same? You're stuck in the past, in—"

"Just because I didn't want to use—"

"Yes!"

Frustrated, she threw up her hands. What was wrong with her? No wonder he was exasperated. She wasn't saying what she really meant, but she didn't dare reveal the one galling fact underlying all the rest of her concerns.

The last thing she was about to admit to Grant Bradley was that she'd gone and fallen in love with him.

TEN

Near two the next morning, Nessa woke out of a sound sleep to the frightening realization that she smelled smoke. For the first few seconds she feared the house was on fire.

Throwing back the covers, she leaped from the bed, slid into the shoes she kept right beside it, and ran out into the hall. Sniffing, her nose in the air, she hesitated. The smoky smell seemed to be only in her room, where the window had been left open a crack to let in the fresh night air. The rain had ended hours earlier and been followed by a stiff breeze that had begun drying things out again.

"What's the matter?" Mary Ellen asked in a sleepy voice. She peeked out of her room, to which she'd returned after one night in Nessa's.

"I smelled smoke. From outdoors, I think, but—"

"I'll wake the others on this floor," Mary Ellen said. "Just to be safe. You take the downstairs."

Nessa didn't argue. Once she was on the lower level, she knocked on Bea and Doug's door, rousing them, then went to check the ashes in the parlor stove. They were safely cold, and the cookstove in the kitchen, though still warm to the touch, was certainly not overheated. She could see only a few embers glowing inside when she lifted one of the heavy cast-iron lids.

Her next thought was of a chimney fire. Hurrying outside by way of the back porch, she glanced toward the roof. Creosote could build up in a chimney or stovepipe and catch unexpectedly, but no plume of flame was shooting up from the top of the house. Hurrying now, for she could once again smell smoke, she circled to the front yard and on around to the other side, where the wraparound porch met the path at the northwest corner of the house. As she broke into a run, Nessa realized what must be burning.

The outhouse was on fire.

The wooden structure was old and its walls bone dry in spite of the recent rain. The smoldering planks suddenly blazed up before her eyes like a bonfire, bright against the night sky.

A shout told her Grant had spotted the conflagration. The sound of footsteps filled the night air, from the barn, from the house. Everyone was awake now and coming outside.

"Brooms," Grant yelled, pointing to her.

Brooms? Then she understood. If they had brooms, they could beat out any falling embers. Twenty yards wasn't quite far enough from the rest of the buildings to be sure they wouldn't catch fire too. She turned and ran back into the house, Mary Ellen at her heels. Moments later they were back, armed and grim-faced, and went to work as backup for the team now operating a bucket brigade from the watering trough.

Grant and Doug made no effort to put the fire out. It was too far along. They concentrated on wetting down spots that had not yet caught. Ash fell like spitting snow, with deceptive gentleness. Glowing spots dotted the ground, most sputtering out as soon as they hit but the odd spark flaring up. Soot and smoke filled the air as well, choking Nessa as she soldiered on. She knew she'd always had a husky voice. After this it would be even deeper for a while. As for the lilac bushes lining the path, they would never be the same.

Fanning out around the burning structure, they watched for any sign that the fire might spread. Three women, three men, Nessa noted. Craig was missing, but she didn't have the leisure to search for him. The look on Jason's face, though, momentarily caught her attention. He looked almost gleeful as he watched the structure burn.

It sputtered and flamed and finally collapsed with a groan of timbers just as they heard the first wail of sirens. Only then did Craig come out of the barn, carrying his cell phone.

"I called the fire department," he announced, unnecessarily, when he reached Nessa's side. In a lower voice, meant for her ears alone, he added, "And the local TV station."

"What? Why?" She kept her words soft, too, but he must have seen the fury in her gaze.

"Why do you think? Never pass up an opportunity, Nessa."

She didn't have time to say anything further to him, and wasn't sure what she would have said if she did. He was right. He was also very, very wrong to have brought Westbrook Farm to the attention of the media.

What would this do to their insurance rates? She couldn't begin to guess. And the fire might make it harder to get funding. The only thing she could think of to do was to fend off the reporter, to put a positive spin on what had happened. Generate good publicity instead of bad.

When the first news team appeared minutes later, she abandoned the last of the firefighting effort to those more skilled and went to meet the press.

Craig was right behind her.

Grant saw them go.

Watching one of the buildings at Westbrook Farm crumble to a mound of debris, even the least of them, was a gut-wrenching experience for him. Turning to discover the woman he thought he

loved in earnest conversation with a television reporter sent a shaft of pain straight to his heart.

He hadn't seen the cameraman and reporter
arrive. He had no idea who had alerted them. But
he had the darkest suspicions when he saw how
cozy both Nessa and Seton were with these unwelcome intruders. He could not help remembering that Nessa had a show up for syndication.
After the childhood she'd had, he couldn't see her
passing up a chance at fame and fortune. And
what was it they said about any publicity being
good publicity?

For Nessa, maybe. For Westbrook Farm? He
doubted it.

Distracted by questions from the local fire
chief and the beginning of the clean up, Grant
managed to block Nessa from his thoughts, but
when all the outsiders had left and their bedrag-
gled-looking group had gathered in the sitting
room, exhaustion plain in the expressions on their
dirty faces, all his doubts rushed back. He didn't
have to tell them that something like this was not
good for the future of the project. He didn't have
the heart to say much at all.

"Okay, it's over and we're all safe," was all he
could manage. "We'll rebuild. But right now I
suggest we all go back to bed and try to catch a
few more hours of sleep."

"Good idea," Seton said, yawning, and headed
off.

The others quickly dispersed, all but Nessa.

Grant didn't look directly at her, but he could sense her presence behind him.

"You have something to say?" he asked, staring hard at the portraits of Ella and Tunis. It would have been a tragedy to lose their house, especially now.

"A problem, I think." She sounded oddly tentative. "How did the fire start?"

What difference did it make? Grant was too tired to think straight. He said the first thing that came to mind. "Turning investigative reporter, are we?"

"Don't be snide, Grant." She was very close to him now. He could smell the smoke in her hair. "Was it an accident?"

His head pounded, a knot of tension throbbing at the back. She was right. There was something odd about the fire, but he didn't like thinking that way. Sarcasm laced his reply. "Well, we couldn't very well have an electrical fire with no wiring. And there haven't been any freak lightning strikes. And mice do not use matches."

"What if someone snuck out for a smoke and didn't completely extinguish the cigarette butt?"

"No one here smokes." Finally, he turned, his eyes locking on Nessa's bright blue gaze.

"Jason does."

Grant raked his filthy hands through his soot-laden hair. Jason? She was accusing Jason?

"I don't mean that business with the pipe," she continued. "He smoked heavily at one time and he still may. I thought the first time I met Jason that he was a chain-smoker. His face shows all the signs. I did a segment—"

"I know he used to smoke." Grant knew Jason well. When Corinne had made her absurd charges against Grant, Jason had been there for him. Jason and Hank. Exhaustion, mental and physical, made him sway on his feet. "If that's what happened, he'd have said so."

"Don't snap at me. I don't like this any better than you do. But I saw Jason's face as he watched the flames. It was gleeful. Almost . . . gloating. And there could be a reason for that. Tell me, Grant. If this project fails, might the theater department profit? Financially, I mean? Are they in line for funding if you lose it?"

He rubbed his eyes with his fists. It was a good guess. It might even be accurate. But how could she suggest the fire might have been deliberately set? He struggled to remember Jason's actions while they fought the blaze. He had thought at the time that the theater professor had hung back, but so had Craig Seton.

"There's a lot of competition in the academic world," Nessa reminded him. "All that publish or perish business. I'm not saying the fire was premeditated. But think about it. We'd been talking about insurance risks. What if Jason was out there, smoking, and the fire started by accident. If he knew he'd benefit from your failure, the temptation would have been enormous to go ahead and let the outhouse burn."

He walked over to the window, once more giving Nessa his back. Dawn wasn't far off. A thin, pale line appeared in the east. He saw it through a haze of smoke. How had the fire gotten such a good start? They'd had a soaking rain only yesterday. And a cigarette butt thrown down the hole wouldn't have continued to burn. That meant a cigarette left burning near the roll of paper on the dry wood of the seat. Not likely by accident. But not Jason. They'd been friends too long. That left him with another ugly suspicion.

"You were the first one to smell smoke," he said to Nessa. "The first one on the scene too. Did you see anything suspicious? Anyone suspicious?"

"No, but when the arson investigator shows up tomorrow . . ." She joined him at the window in time to see the first pale pink light of dawn appear on the distant horizon beyond the pond. "That is, later today," she corrected herself, "I think he should be told."

"That would put you in the spotlight again."

She started. "What are you saying, Grant?" Reflected in the glass, her expression was puzzled, but he told himself she was used to projecting whatever emotion she wanted.

"How do I know you didn't start the fire?" he asked bluntly. "Makes as much sense as blaming

Jason. After all, you've gotten something out of it already. You can't deny that."

"Don't be absurd." She put one hand on his arm.

He shook it off. "Seton was quick to play news spotter."

"He thought alerting the media would be good for my career." Affronted, she held herself rigid. "He didn't stop to consider the damage it might do to the project. However, I think we managed to put a positive spin on things."

Grant couldn't tell if she was upset because Seton had called the TV station or because he had questioned her role in the fire and its aftermath. Maybe she wouldn't commit arson, but he wasn't so sure about Seton, and he could not exonerate her of taking advantage of the situation after the fact. She would profit from the exposure Westbrook Farm was about to get in the media.

He had no reason to trust any woman's loyalty to him, he reminded himself. No reason to expect fair treatment from someone who made her living on television.

Although the parlor stove had been lit and had made the room comfortably warm, Nessa suddenly shivered. For the first time, Grant noticed what she was wearing. On this particular night, she'd chosen to sleep in the frilly lace and linen confection he'd chosen for Katie. It was ruined now, blackened with soot, but it must have been an extremely effective look on camera.

His darkest suspicions deepened.

"Let's say it was arson," she suggested. "Could it have been someone from outside? Is there anyone you can think of who might want to sabotage the project?"

"Oh, sure," he drawled, past sarcastic now and into sardonic. "Someone who doesn't want Westbrook Farm to open. Let me see. Your assistant keeps pointing out that not everyone's crazy about all this history stuff. Maybe some poor grad student who thinks he's going to be stuck living here for the whole summer decided to take the easy way out."

"There must be *some* explanation."

Grant immediately thought of one. So simple. So stupid. So . . . laughable. An edgy chuckle escaped him, making her look at him askance. He shrugged. "Maybe the fire *was* set. I suppose it could have been a prank."

"Some prank!"

He left the window and bent to rearrange the wood in the parlor stove, more for something to do than because it needed his attention. "I remember my father talking about one Fourth of July when he was a kid. He and some of his buddies set fire to one of the comfort stations at a highway rest stop. Everyone thought it was pretty funny. Other kids, anyway. The same sort of kids who, a generation earlier, thought it was a hoot to turn the privy over when there was someone inside."

"That's funny?" Nessa sounded doubtful. She'd followed him across the room and stood just behind him, watching his every move.

He shoved his glasses back into place and straightened, but he didn't turn to face her. "Maybe it's a guy thing. And maybe I'm so tired, I'm punchy. But right now I'd rather laugh than cry."

Nessa stared at the broad back he presented to her. Grant's back in Simon's torn and dirty white cotton shirt. The words were right, but he wasn't laughing now, and neither was she.

He thought her capable of setting a fire, or of conspiring with Craig to do it. How could he?

But she knew very well how he could. She supposed she couldn't even blame him for being suspicious, given his past experience and the fact that if Craig hadn't called them, no one from the media would have bothered to show up at such a remote fire scene. Still, his distrust hurt.

"What happens next?" she asked.

His expression was stony when he finally faced her. "Whatever or whoever started the fire, we were lucky it didn't spread to the house or barn. One of us might have been hurt, even killed. The fire marshall will have to do a thorough investigation. If someone was responsible, it will come out."

The sound of a throat being cleared drew their attention to the door to the hall, to Jason. Nessa couldn't tell how long he'd been there, but he'd obviously overheard Grant's last comment.

"The fire may have been my fault," he said. "I was having a smoke out there earlier. I thought I'd extinguished the cigarette, but I could have been careless." He lifted his hands in a helpless, apologetic gesture.

Nessa stared hard at him. Had he been lurking in the hallway long enough to have overheard her voice her suspicions? Was he confessing to avert an investigation into his real motives? Or had it really been the accident he claimed?

Sadness settled over her as she listened to Grant and Jason converse in quiet tones. No matter what had really happened, Grant resented both what she'd just said and what she'd done earlier in talking to that reporter. He wasn't the least bit grateful for her attempt to help with the press.

"We'll start rebuilding right after breakfast," she heard Grant tell Jason. He didn't seem nearly as upset with the other man as he had been with her.

"Sorry, Grant," Jason apologized again. "These things happen."

As soon as Jason left the sitting room, Grant turned to Nessa. "I don't want you mentioning this to the arson investigator."

She bristled at his tone. Would he have asked the same thing of Jason if their roles had been reversed? Shaking off the oppressive tiredness that threatened to swamp her, she drew herself up straighter and stared into his dark eyes. "Why not?"

"Because I intend to handle it myself. I'll talk to him. So will Jason. Any more of us and it will only muddy the waters."

"But—"

"You didn't say anything about the fire being deliberately set to that reporter, did you?"

"No, of course not."

He glared at her. "You do that well."

"What?"

"Artful confusion." He sounded cynical. "What now? Are you planning to apologize too? Offer to make it all better?"

She ignored the second part of his question, with its overlay of sexual innuendo. "What, exactly, would I be apologizing for? Waking up in time to sound the alarm?"

"The smoke alarms would have alerted us." They *had* started to blare soon after Nessa and Mary Ellen woke everyone, but Nessa wasn't about to have her contribution discounted so cavalierly.

"Every second counted." She put her hand on his arm again as he started to move away from her. "If sparks had reached the house—"

Abruptly, he turned and caught her to him, his fingers pressing into her upper arms with bruising force. "Sparks?" he asked in a husky, ravaged voice. Anger and suspicion burned in his eyes, but so did barely banked desire. "It's too late, Nessa.

You've gotten your publicity. I hope you're happy with your syndication deal. I'm sure this will sew it up for you."

Hurt, she fought as he started to lower his head to kiss her. He backed off fast enough when she kicked him.

"Guess you got what you were really after," he said.

"Believe me, the last thing I wanted was notoriety."

"Believe you? Give me one good reason why I should"

She wanted to scream it at him. *Because I love you!*

Instead she let him walk away.

ELEVEN

By noon, Grant and Jason had dug the trench for a new privy and started construction. It would not have the aesthetic appeal of the flagstone walk and the lilac bushes, but it would be functional by nightfall.

The hard labor helped calm the almost irrational rage Grant had felt earlier, but it did nothing to dim his suspicions of Nessa. He'd been a fool for a woman. Again. He should have known right from the start that she was not for him.

He was just glad they didn't have any television sets at Westbrook Farm. At least he didn't have to see and hear proof of her perfidy.

Grant stopped work only twice, once to talk to the arson investigator, the second time to deal with a harried Hank Gilbert, who made a flying visit to the farm before rushing back to institute "damage control" of his own kind.

This project would not fail, Grant vowed as he sweated and slaved. Doug came out to help them, but Seton was conspicuously absent. By the time the new privy was ready—a single-hole model this time but with the requisite tight-fitting door and grilled air vents—Grant still did not want to go back into the house and face Nessa. Instead he washed off in the water trough, made a brief stop in his bedroom in the barn for a fresh shirt, and set out for the pond.

He had an hour or more of daylight left. He could walk around the water's edge and up the hill and spend a short time in solitude, contemplating the dig for Indian artifacts he'd one day undertake at various sites on the Westbrook property. And lose himself in work. Forget women.

Forget one woman in particular.

Nessa watched him go.

They couldn't let it end this way, she thought. Tomorrow she was scheduled to return to her old life. The only link between them would be the documentary, which she could edit and turn over to Hank without ever seeing Grant again.

No. Unacceptable. He'd been hurting and had struck out at her. She couldn't like that reaction, but she could understand it, at least a little. She needed to tell him so.

With Bea's help, she packed a picnic basket and set out across the field. The setting sun behind her showed her the way, although she didn't know exactly where to find Grant. She assumed that from the top of the hill she would be able to spot him. There were trees, but they were not thick. And she had a feeling he might have headed for that so-called Indian cave he'd told her about. She could look for any outcropping of rock.

Her self-confidence slipped a bit when she completed her climb and stopped, breathing hard, to survey the hillside. She saw no sign of movement anywhere. And nothing that looked like a cave. Belatedly, she remembered that here in the boonies there were snakes and other unpleasant critters.

She looked back the way she'd come. The sun was beginning to disappear behind the farmhouse. A beautiful sight. A scary sight. She hadn't thought before she began her trek that it might be difficult to make her way back after dark. She'd be lucky if she didn't break her fool neck trying to descend the hill and cross the field without a light.

Grant appeared as if out of nowhere, making her suck in her breath with an audible gasp as she whirled to face him.

"What are you doing here?" he demanded.

"I brought you supper," she blurted, extending the basket toward him.

"That wasn't necessary."

The sun was at her back but fell full on Grant's face. She studied his expression and decided to take that puzzled frown as a good sign. It was certainly an improvement over the suspicion and disillusionment she'd seen there at dawn.

"We need to clear the air between us," she said.

A tiny smile curved his lips, but it was not the product of mirth. "Seems to me I've heard that line before. Aren't you afraid I'll dump you in the pond or feed you to the snakes?"

"Of course not. That would be terrible publicity. You need me alive and on your side." Bravado imbued her words, but inside she was shaking. So much depended upon this encounter. Her whole future.

"Your kind of help is going to flush this place right down the toilet."

"Jason's cigarette started the fire. I had nothing to do with that."

"Maybe not, but you sure were quick to take advantage of the opportunity."

"Opportunity for what, Grant? I was trying to make the best of a bad situation." Why wouldn't he listen? Stubborn, opinionated man! She couldn't imagine why she wanted to keep him in her life.

"Did your syndication offer come through?"

She faltered. She wasn't about to lie, but she'd have given a lot not to have had Craig's cell phone ring just before she set out from the house. "Yes. It did."

"Congratulations."

"I haven't made any decision yet. I may not

accept." Probably wouldn't, in fact, but she didn't suppose Grant would believe her if she told him so.

"Don't tell me you're considering turning it down because of me."

Nessa opened her mouth and closed it again. She *was* going to turn it down. She'd always been inclined to turn it down. Her feelings on the matter had hardly anything to do with Grant.

"You are a most exasperating man," she said. "Sit. We might as well eat, since I lugged this food all the way up the hill." Maybe feeding him would make him mellow enough to listen to her.

Suiting her action to her words, she settled herself on a patch of brown grass that didn't look conspicuously damp and opened the wicker basket. She experienced a fleeting regret that they did not have a sleeping bag to sit on this time. The ground was dry enough, but chilly and uneven beneath her bottom. She also found herself wishing she'd worn one of Katie's dresses. All those layers of fabric did have the advantage of providing both padding and warmth.

"There is no point in prolonging this," Grant said. He didn't sit, but he did accept the sandwich she thrust toward him.

"Prolonging what?" She pulled out a stoneware container of spring water. Their nineteenth-century supplies didn't include a thermos bottle for coffee.

"This impossible relationship. We have nothing in common but great sex and brains that seem to serve as storehouses for miscellaneous trivia. It's over, Nessa. Tomorrow you go your way and I'll go mine. End of story."

Glad of the rapidly gathering dusk, Nessa bent over the basket again to hide incipient tears. If that was the way he wanted to end things, she wasn't going to beg. But she'd hoped—

She cut off the thought, half formed. She was a realist, practical to a fault. With brisk, efficient motions she gathered up the picnic supper she'd just laid out—the water bottle, slices of cake, two apples—and closed the basket once more. She'd tried. She'd come all the way up there to talk to him. It wasn't her fault he was too stubborn to listen.

"Where are you going now?"

She didn't answer. She couldn't. If she tried to speak, he'd hear the tears she was all but choking on.

Turning her back on him, she made her way rapidly down the hill and around the pond. The sun's light gave out on her just as she passed the boathouse.

Cautiously, she picked her way across the meadow. The rough ground was treacherous, but she barely registered her own stumbling steps. To her chagrin, she'd begun crying in earnest. A searing pain slammed into her chest. Either she was severely winded from sprinting from the hilltop or her heart was breaking in two. She increased her speed, almost running now. What did it matter if she stepped in a chuckhole and broke her leg as well?

Dazed, despairing, she followed the flickering light of a lantern set out near the water trough. Oblivious to all around her, she staggered the last few yards and fell to her knees to scoop up great handfuls of cold water. She dashed it against her face, heedless of the spatters on her clothing, determined to wash away every trace of her weakness.

She was behaving like a ninnyhammer again. Intolerable! She was a modern woman. She could handle . . . disappointment.

Straightening her spine, Nessa reached for one of the towels Bea customarily left by the trough. She told herself she was strong and that no man was worth crying over.

Only when she'd finished drying her face and hands did she realize Craig was nearby, waiting for her in the shadows by the barn. She swore softly. He'd obviously seen her return, witnessed her weak, self-pitying tears.

"I'm sorry, Nessa," he said, confirming her suspicions.

In spite of her desire to stand alone, she let him put his arms around her. The moment he touched her, she realized she needed consoling. Just this once, she accepted Craig's offer of comfort.

❖━━━━❖

Grant walked around the corner of the barn and froze at the sight of Nessa in Seton's arms. He'd followed her down the hill, his thoughts in turmoil. He hadn't been able to stop himself. But now a darker emotion took over. He wanted to tear Nessa away from the other man. He wanted to beat Seton to a bloody pulp.

He did nothing.

True, he'd sent her away, but she'd run straight into Seton's arms. She wouldn't be there if she didn't want to be. She'd clearly made her choice. He told himself it was better this way. He and Nessa could never have made a future together. She had much more in common with Craig Seton.

He watched as the two of them slowly walked off toward the house. He did not go after her.

But his heart felt as if it were breaking in two.

"Watch out for the knickknack shelf," Nessa warned. Craig had almost backed into it.

"Whatnot." Watching from the doorway, Grant corrected her choice of words in a pedantic voice.

"Whatever."

"It's a specific period name. Shelves meant for curios and bric-a-brac. The Westbrooks probably had figurines and shells. Peacock feathers and coral were popular too."

"Go away, Grant. I need to reshoot this one sequence before I pack up and leave Westbrook Farm." The plan had been to be on the road by noon, and it was already ten. She needed to talk to Grant before she left, but not now. Work, she told herself, must come first. It always did. Always should.

"It's wasted effort if you aren't accurate."

Rounding on him, she lowered her camera. "I can't imagine our ancestors were any more careful of the words they used in speech than we are. I mean, people who have been in my business for a long time frequently say film when they mean videotape, but the rest of us know what they mean. It isn't a big deal."

"Maybe that's the difference between your profession and mine." *Between you and me,* he seemed to be adding as he took a step closer to her. "I prefer to be exact. Take the term chamber set."

"A bed, dresser, and chest of drawers?" she guessed. She set the camera on the settee and glared at him, her hands fisted on her hips.

"A chamber set refers to a basin and large-mouthed pitcher for washing, a cup for brushing the teeth, and a chamber pot. Chamber sets were provided in hotel rooms from about 1830 and soon caught on in private homes." He stood, arms akimbo, staring back at her.

"More than I really needed to know," she muttered. And more evidence of how little they had in common. She sighed.

"I want this documentary to be accurate," he said.

"Fine. Now can we get back to what I was doing?"

"Of course." All of a sudden, he sounded agreeable, and her eyes narrowed in suspicion. The man had barely spoken to her since that miserable scene on the hill the previous evening and then he'd reverted to being the stuffy professor of a week earlier, and now he was . . . what? Trying to be charming?

Bea's voice reached them clearly, although she was in the kitchen. "Are they at it again?"

It was Craig who answered her. He'd left the sitting room, and Nessa hadn't even noticed. All her attention had been focused on Grant.

"You need to ask?" He sounded disgruntled. "When they come up for air, tell Nessa I've left."

An uncomfortable silence settled over the sitting room.

"I guess they knew we were involved," Grant said. His dark eyes bored into her, but she couldn't begin to guess his thoughts.

"I guess they did."

"So much for discretion." As if he found it too painful to continue looking at her, he turned his head toward the whatnot. "That last shot ought to work. Clumsy farmhand in the house. Add a little humor to the thing."

Blinking in surprise, Nessa absently picked up her camera once more. He was right. He was usually right, damn him. Even about the fact that the two of them had no future together.

"Bea said you were looking for me earlier."

She cleared her throat. "Yes. I thought you ought to know that I asked a few questions last night and this morning. I wanted to clear up some loose ends."

"Go on."

"Craig did come here to convince me to abandon the project. When he realized I was committed to staying, he signed on in the hope of finding a way to get me to leave ahead of schedule. He says he didn't start out intending sabotage, but when I had trouble with the batteries, he thought he'd found the means to speed me on my way. One battery ran down. One failed. The trouble with the others was Craig's doing."

A quick glance at Grant's eyes told her he was thinking of the afternoon they had spent in his apartment while the batteries recharged. How ironic that they owed such a memorable interlude to Craig Seton.

"What else did your assistant do?" he asked. "Maybe slip something into Mary Ellen's food? Torch the privy?"

Glaring, she spat out the rest of what she'd intended to say. "Food poisoning was Mary Ellen's little game. Are you too dense to see that, even now? She was jealous, Grant. She wanted your attention."

"So she made herself sick? I can't—"

"Believe it? Believe it, Grant. Not that she was actually ill. She faked her symptoms. She's a very good little actress. She and Jason should get together. Form a touring theater troupe."

Nessa heard her words come out with much more vehemence than she'd intended and was appalled. She struggled to regain control of her emotions. What did it matter if Mary Ellen had a crush on her professor? It certainly wasn't any of Nessa's concern. Not anymore.

Then their eyes met. She saw a spark of something in his dark and smoldering gaze. More than a spark. She felt an answering response, too, a tightening deep in her womb. She swayed toward him, but caught the impulse in time.

Nessa shook her head, trying to force her mind to work with its usual efficiency. This conversation was going nowhere. She had to get away from him, away from the maelstrom of emotions he made her feel. A part of her wanted nothing more than to fling herself into his arms and ask him to let her stay with him forever. The more rational side of her brain knew that even a brief love affair between them would never work.

They'd be doomed from the start. With all their differences, they'd soon grow apart. The career conflicts would escalate. Neither one of them was any damned good at compromise. Sooner or later, one or both of them would abandon the attempt.

She'd be alone again, with only bitter memories for company.

Something she didn't need.

Something she didn't want.

Better to walk out of his life before he could walk out of hers.

"That's it," she said. "That's all I wanted to tell you before I left."

"Are you sure you knew nothing about Seton's plan to call the TV station when the fire started?" he asked. "I saw the two of you last night. You looked pretty . . . tight to me."

"I've answered that one before. I won't repeat myself."

And she wouldn't defend or explain her relationship with Craig again, either. Grant didn't trust her. That was painfully obvious. If she'd had any faint hope that they might have a future together, it flickered and died at his harsh words.

He raked his hands through his hair. How had she ever found that gesture endearing? "Forget Seton for the moment," he said. "I know how important your career is to you. I don't—"

"What does my career have to do with anything!" First he was jealous of Craig. Now he was jealous of her job?

"Everything. You put it first, don't you? Ahead of everything else?"

She couldn't deny the charge. "Just as you put your project first. No compromises."

"No compromises," he agreed.

That seemed to say it all.

"Good-bye, Grant." Nessa hoisted her camera, using it as a barrier between them. "It's been an experience. Seems you were right the other day about Westbrook Farm. It's a nice place to visit, but I wouldn't want to live here."

TWELVE

"Just look at it, Hank. It's all wrong." Grant glared at the television screen in his office at Sidwell College. What was most wrong was that Nessa did not appear anywhere in the footage they'd just watched.

"I'm looking," Hank said. "You know what I see? I see someone searching for an excuse to confront the person who shot this video. Well, go for it, man. Why torture yourself?"

He confronted her all the time, Grant thought ruefully. In the weeks since he'd last seen her in person, Nessa had haunted the office and his apartment with her presence. And the diner too. He couldn't be in any of those places without thinking of her. And at night she invaded his bed, keeping him awake, tormenting him in dreams, making him restless and needy. He regretted the way he'd behaved that last day at Westbrook

Farm. It was as if he'd been trying to drive her away before she had a chance to tell him there was no room for him in her life.

It didn't seem as if they had much to build on, but he'd damned himself for a fool more times than he wanted to count for not giving them a fighting chance to find out for sure.

"She turned down that syndication offer," Hank said.

"Why?"

"Why don't you ask her? Give her a call. Drop by."

"Strongtown and Syracuse aren't exactly next door to each other."

"They aren't at opposite ends of the universe either. Taffy and I manage to see a lot of each other." Hank ran one finger beneath the edge of his collar, as if his tie suddenly felt too tight. "We're talking about getting married. Maybe."

"She'll move here?"

Hank's expression told Grant he'd never even considered that he might be the one to uproot himself, to change jobs. Some jobs, Grant thought, tied you to a place. As his did to Sidwell College and Westbrook Farm.

If Nessa had turned down the syndication deal, it could only mean she wanted to stay where she was. In Syracuse. On the other side of the state. And New York was a *big* state.

The reality of the physical distance between

them was reinforced ten days later, when Grant made the trip from Strongtown.

She lived in a condominium in the best section of Syracuse. Figured. He rang the buzzer by her unit number, but he was already sure this had been a wasted trip.

Her voice on the phone had been curt and businesslike. Professional. At least that boded well for the content of the final videotape. Her reputation was at stake here too. But he had to admit, at least to himself, that if she hadn't called and asked him to meet with her to discuss the changes he wanted, he'd have found another way to see her again. He saw no hope for them, no future together, but he wanted—no, needed, to talk to her one more time.

The next few hours were likely to be difficult. Just as the last weeks had been. For dreaming of her, he didn't think he'd had a full night's sleep since she left Westbrook Farm.

The door opened abruptly. Nessa stood framed in the portal, as breathtakingly beautiful as he remembered, even if she was casually dressed in a sweat suit, her hair tied back in a stubby ponytail and not a speck of makeup in sight.

"Nessa," he said.

"Grant."

"Are you going to let me in?"

"I don't suppose I have any choice." She stood back, waving him through, and he got his first good look at the place where she lived.

His heart sank. In spite of the antique Turkish Oshak rug covering the cherrywood floor, the foyer screamed "modern" at him. What he saw of the living room reinforced the impression. It was dominated by a huge brick and granite fireplace. Arranged atop a pale beige rug were several uncomfortably small lounge chairs and a coffee table inlaid with burled wood. An old English walnut chest did flank one fireside chair, and an antique dresser he suspected had come from Wales had been placed against the inner wall, but the overall effect was about as far removed from the decor at Westbrook Farm as the space shuttle was from a plow.

"Nice place," he said.

She murmured a thank-you as she led him past the master bedroom to her at-home office. There his sense of being in a luxury condominium increased. The room was dedicated to work and the tools of her trade occupied every available surface, but overhead was an immense skylight.

In one corner two plain wooden chairs faced a television set hooked up to a VCR. "Sit," she invited. "I'll show you what I've done."

He sat. She pushed a button that shuttered the skylight and plunged the room into semidarkness. She gave him no opportunity for small talk, and since the project was important to him, he went along with her. Business first. Then . . . whatever.

An hour later when the video ended, they sat

in silence. The revised documentary was excellent, all he could have hoped for and more. Aside from a few minor details, easily fixed, which he'd pointed out to her during the viewing, she'd produced precisely what Westbrook Farm needed to draw both interest and investors.

In this version, she'd done the narration herself, and every word she uttered had sung with conviction, as if she had a deep and abiding affection for the project.

"I don't know what to say, Nessa."

"How about whether you liked it or not?" She sounded testy.

"Of course I liked it. What's not to like? You did a magnificent job."

Mollified, she busied herself removing the tape from the VCR. She avoided meeting his eyes as she mumbled her thanks for the compliment.

"What happens now?" he asked.

"Now I fix those few glitches, make copies, and ship them off to Hank."

So his part was done, Grant concluded. She acted as if she couldn't wait for him to leave.

Why *was* he sticking around? The environment in her office was nearly as foreign to him as the decor in the other rooms. Seeing her lifestyle made him certain they were as far apart as he'd thought. She had her whole future here, and he couldn't see her giving it up for anything less than a lucrative syndication deal. What little she'd told him of her early years only reinforced that conviction.

On the other hand, she'd understood precisely what he wanted in the documentary. They thought alike on that subject.

"Well, that's it then," she said, ushering him into the hall. As they passed her bedroom door, her steps faltered.

"How about a guided tour?" he asked, his voice suddenly as husky as hers.

"The only thing you haven't seen already is the bedroom."

He waited. The air began to shimmer between them. Liquid heat. He heard her long intake of breath and kept listening as she held it. One beat. Two. Then he sealed it in with his lips, and when the kiss ended, she exhaled in a whoosh and a sputter.

"I've missed you," he whispered.

Nessa's heart turned over. "I've missed you too," she confessed.

The last weeks had seemed endless. Every moment that she'd spent reliving her time at Westbrook Farm while she edited the videotape had been sweet agony. She'd frozen frames more times than she could count just to stare at the face now only a few inches away from hers.

She wanted him.

She wanted him almost enough to consider compromising.

"I hated the way we parted," she murmured.

"It's not the best memory of the week."

"We could replace it with a better one." There. She'd given him an opening. It was up to Grant to make the next move.

He cooperated beautifully.

Once they were in each other's arms, it was as if they'd never been apart. The differences vanished. The obstacles were forgotten. For a few stolen hours, they lost themselves in loving, shutting out reality, ignoring the rest of the world. It might have been any century, for what they found in each other's arms was timeless.

But dreams end, even the good ones. Morning comes. Nessa awoke to find Grant studying her with a somber expression on his face. In silence, they made love one last time, then rose and dressed. She prepared breakfast for them in her ultramodern kitchen.

"What *did* happen with that syndication deal?" he asked over a final cup of coffee.

"I turned it down."

"Why?"

"I like what I'm doing now." She waited for him to inquire what that might be, because what she was "doing now" was working on starting a brand-new career.

"Thought that might be it." He stood, setting his cup aside. "I have to be going. It's a long drive home."

"How's the new Katie doing?"

"You'd have to ask the new Simon."

"Aren't you supervising the live-ins?"

"I'm concentrating on an earlier century now."

The Indian project, she remembered. She had done some research herself. Found out who Tom Quick was. She didn't tell Grant. If he couldn't compromise, why should she? Instead she walked him to the door, determined to be stoic, to send him on his way with only good memories.

"Drive safely," she said.

He kissed her. On the cheek. Then he was gone.

First, she cried.

Then she broke a vase she'd never liked much anyway, flinging it against the fireplace with a fine vengeance. Her emotional outburst over, she sank into a chair and took a good, hard look at what she wanted out of life.

Not things, she realized. She might once have needed to accumulate trophies to prove she'd succeeded, but she no longer required that kind of material reinforcement. All she needed was a purpose. A goal. An agenda for her future. Well, she had that, didn't she? She had her new business venture. A woman didn't have to have a man to be complete. So what if she'd spent the last few weeks dreaming of white lace and promises? Absence had made her heart grow fonder. That was all. Now she'd seen him again; now she could forget him.

❦━━━━━━━━━❦

Nessa tried very hard to forget Grant. She had plenty to keep her busy over the next few months.

Grant tried to forget Nessa. He had a great deal to occupy his time from May to August.

Neither of them succeeded in forgetting a thing.

Three times a year, the president of Sidwell College threw a gala reception for those faculty members who'd had new publications or had otherwise distinguished themselves. To the dismay of the English department, August's honors list included a classified employee, a lowly part-timer on the library staff who'd had the audacity to write and sell a mystery novel.

Grant found the novelist by far the most interesting person at the reception, until a vision in an electric-blue dress walked through the door.

"Isn't that Vanessa Dare?" his companion asked. "What on earth is she doing here?"

"Oh, didn't you know?" Hank Gilbert joined them just in time to hear the question. "She's being honored along with Grant here for her work on the Westbrook Farm project. We arranged for her to make a documentary about our preparations for opening, but she took it upon herself to see that copies of the videotape got to every influential contact she's developed over the years. It's due to her efforts that we've landed new outside funding."

Grabbing Hank's arm, Grant dragged him to one side, rudely leaving the librarian to think what she would. "What investors? What's going on, Hank?"

His old friend feigned innocence, but not very well. After a moment he gave up the effort and grinned. "Thought you'd be pleased. That non-profit corporation we talked about is all sewed up, thanks to Nessa. She's been a busy gal since she left Westbrook Farm."

"I'm sure it profits her career as well."

"I'm sure it does, but she also seems to have a real fondness for your little project."

Watching Nessa charm every man in the place was excruciatingly painful for Grant. She was more beautiful, more glamorous, than he'd ever seen her before. The dress, in addition to matching the exact shade of her eyes, was made of some sort of clingy material that emphasized every luscious curve of breast and hip. The cowl neck was demure enough in front, drooping only to show a choker that matched her earrings, but in the back . . . When she turned, he swallowed hard. He was staring at an expanse of bare skin that dipped down almost to her waist, a sight that made him remember, in vivid detail, what lay just south of that line. Dimples. One on each side.

His body hardened in a rush, and he nearly groaned aloud. Had she worn that dress solely to torment him? Did she somehow guess that he regularly woke in the night, aching for her? She'd been part of his life for one week in April and a single night in May, but those memories seemed to have burned themselves into his mind. Not a day had passed that he hadn't thought of going to her again, but each time he'd argued himself out of contacting her. Too much stood between them.

Without realizing it, he moved across the room to her, heedless of anyone who stood in his way. He didn't even hear the president speak his name. Nothing existed for him but Nessa.

"Hello, Grant," she said, smiling, when he reached her side.

"Nessa. You look . . . well."

They exchanged small talk. He had no idea what he said or what she answered. He was too lost in the sound of her sexy, low-pitched voice.

Only when he realized she was gazing up at him expectantly with those unique electric-blue eyes, did he gather she'd asked him a question. "I'm sorry. What did you say?"

Her smile dazzled him, but this time he forced himself to concentrate on her words. "I wondered if we could get a breath of fresh air. It's horribly crowded and stuffy in here."

He led her out through French doors onto a stone-flagged terrace overlooking the little artificial lake. A full moon sent light dancing on the smooth surface.

"Thanks," she said, leaning back against a low

redbrick wall. "I can't handle more than about twenty minutes of one of these things without wishing I were somewhere else."

He blinked at her in surprise. He felt the same way. Did she mean what she'd said or was she just making an excuse to talk to him alone? His heart speeded up. Either way, the possibilities were appealing. "You aren't comfortable in this kind of situation?"

"A formal reception, full of high-muck-a-mucks? Not really. Something we have in common, I think."

He nodded.

"Not the only thing, either." She was watching him intently, and he couldn't tear his gaze away from her. "We both like to be in charge, to direct, as it were. Neither of us wants to be the star but we sure do relish being the mover and shaker behind the scenes."

"I'm not sure I understand what you mean. You're certainly a star."

"Not anymore." She took a deep breath. "I haven't had my own show since May, Grant. I resigned." Her smile was shaky. "Craig took over as host. He's doing quite well at it. People seem to respond to all that superficial charm."

"He did show up well on camera in your documentary."

"So did Mary Ellen. I'm surprised I haven't seen her here."

"She got her degree in June. She's in the graduate program at Harvard now."

He didn't want to talk about Mary Ellen. Or Seton.

"What are you doing, then," he asked, "if you aren't on TV?"

"Since the last time we met, I've made quite a few changes in my life. For one thing, I started a small, independent production company. In order to finance it, I sold my condo and its contents."

Shock held him momentarily silent. She'd sold all those expensive furnishings? He'd kept imagining her in that setting, telling himself that was where she belonged and that because she did, he'd never fit into her world.

"Where are you living?"

"On the road. Literally. I'm in a RV with all my equipment. Before the snow flies I'll have to find a snug little house or apartment. It could be anywhere. Anywhere at all. I'm open to suggestions."

Stunned by what she'd said, and by what she'd left unsaid, he stared blindly at the lake. At first he didn't know how to respond, but the small body of water made him think of another place.

"I prefer the view of our pond," he whispered. "We could be looking at it in less than an hour."

"I'd like that."

They were united in the mutual desire to shake the posh party and head for Westbrook

Farm. How much more they might agree upon, he didn't dare ask.

"No one's there tonight," he said as they drove out of the parking lot and left the campus.

"I know. I saw Bea and Doug a bit ago at the party. She told me they don't plan to return until tomorrow. *Late* tomorrow."

On the way to Luzon, Nessa told him more about her production company and the first small projects she'd undertaken. She was already building a solid reputation for creating short features and advertising videos.

"Westbrook Farm made it all possible," she said.

Grant answered by sharing Bea and Doug's anecdotes from the first summer of "live-ins" at the farm. They had not been without minor glitches, but had ended successfully enough to guarantee many more seasons to come, especially when combined with the new funding.

"And your archaeological dig?" she asked.

"Scheduled to start next spring. Want to film it?"

"I'd love nothing better."

"Nothing?"

"Well, almost nothing."

They'd reached the farm.

For Grant the walk up from the parking area to the house was fraught with last-minute doubts, but the moment they set foot inside the familiar hallway, Nessa turned and put her arms around him, nestling her cheek against his chest, giving him ample reassurance that she was not going to change her mind.

"Is my old room free?" she asked. "I've been wondering since the first night here what it would be like to share that bed with you."

"It's free. Bea and Doug elected to stay downstairs, mostly because of Bea's arthritis."

He opened the door to the stairwell and guided her upward. They didn't speak again until they'd entered the front room and he'd lit one of the lamps.

"Oh, that wonderful big bed," she said with a sigh of pleasure. "I don't suppose I could steal it away to wherever I end up living?"

"It's part of a set," he said, taking her into his arms.

"With the dresser and chest of—"

"With me. If you want the bed, you can have it, but you'll have to take me too." He swallowed hard. "I love you, Nessa."

"I love you too."

He hugged her. "Thank God. I've been miserable without you."

They tumbled together onto the bed and were too busy relearning each other's bodies to speak again for some time, not until there came a moment when they both remembered protection.

"Do you have—?"

He cut off the question with a kiss. She could

feel his smile against her lips and opened her eyes, questioning him with a look. Against her breasts, his chest was quivering. Shaking.

"You're trying not to laugh," she accused him.

"Sorry."

"I'm not objecting." She felt answering tugs at the corners of her mouth. "I just want to share the joke."

"Not funny. Not really."

"What?" She caught a strand of his chest hair between her teeth and tugged until she was sure she had his attention.

In retaliation, he kissed her thoroughly, leaving her limp and wanting beneath him before he answered. "I was on the Internet a few weeks ago. I came across a Web site for a company that manufactures one of your favorite products. And there was this order form, for a free sample."

She was slow to understand him, but then it hit her, and she giggled. "You ordered a female condom? *You?*"

"Me. In my own name. And I read all the information on the Web site too." He had to struggle to keep a straight face. "You were right. It is a viable alternative. In fact, I think I'm actually looking forward to trying it out. Sometime. Not tonight, though. Tonight I have other plans."

If Nessa had needed any confirmation that she had made the right decision, she had it now. Her stuffy, old-fashioned professor could compromise, just as she could, when finding middle ground was important enough.

And he could laugh.

"Oh, I do love you," she told him.

He became serious again. "You said you could live anywhere. Live with me, Nessa. Marry me?"

"Yes," she whispered.

She caught his hand as he started to open the foil-wrapped packet he'd extracted from the wallet he carried in the pocket of his twentieth-century suit. She looked up at him, feeling herself melt inside. "I've heard there's this tried-and-true method for starting a family. Some couples consider it when they're planning to get married."

He stilled above her.

Had she gone too far? Maybe it was too soon to mention having babies together.

Then she realized he was smiling, a radiant thousand-watt dazzler. He didn't say a word. He didn't have to. He tossed the unnecessary protection aside and began to make sweet love to her.

By the time he slid into her welcoming heat, truly flesh to flesh for the first time, she knew she'd been right to accept his proposal. They were going to fit into each other's lives just as perfectly as they fit each other's bodies. A true partnership. Any compromises they had to make would not be difficult at all. Not when they were motivated by love.

Grant echoed her thoughts perfectly some

time later, when they lay spent in each other's arms, laughing softly in sheer delight with themselves.

"I will be happy in any century," he whispered, "as long as I'm with you."

THE EDITORS' CORNER

Ladies, step back! This July, LOVESWEPT is hotter than ever, with a month full of beguiling heroes and steamy romance. We managed to capture four Rebels with a Cause for your reading pleasure. There's Jack, a rough-and-tough detective with a glint in his eye; Luke, an architect who has to prove his innocence to win the heart of his woman; Clint, an FBI renegade with a score to settle; and Mitch, an ex–Navy Seal who's determined to earn back the life he left behind.

Beautiful Alex Sheridan and sexy Luke Morgan pack a lifetime of passion into **JUST ONE NIGHT**, LOVESWEPT #898, Eve Gaddy's sexy tale of two strangers who are trying to forget the past. As an officer on the Dallas bomb squad, Alex is called in to investigate the bombing of a construction site. All leads point to Luke, the architect on the project: he's a trained explosives expert; a large amount of money mysteriously shows up in his account; *and* he's the son of a convicted terrorist. As the hunt for the bomber continues, Alex and Luke are in too deep to keep their relationship on a professional basis. Alex had feared she'd never be able to trust herself again, but will Luke convince her that her instincts about him are right? Eve Gaddy pulls at the heartstrings in this moving story of a man who's backed against a wall and the woman who's willing to risk everything to save him.

In **A SCENT OF EDEN,** LOVESWEPT #899, Cynthia Powell demonstrates the delicious power of unlikely attractions. When Eden Wellbourne's fiancé goes missing, it's up to her to find the culprit. To that end, she hires Jack Rafferty, a man who is reputed to have an unmatched expertise in locating missing persons, a man who is clearly living on the edge. Meanwhile, Jack is having the second-worst day of his life, and he's definitely not in the mood to deal with the uptown girl standing on his doorstep. With his cash flow at an all-time low, however, he reluctantly decides to take on her case. Both are confused at the physical pull they feel toward each other, but neither wants to act on it first. When a break-in convinces Eden her own life is in danger, she turns to Jack for more than just his people-finding talents. Everything comes up roses when Cynthia Powell crosses a down-on-his-luck tough guy with a perfume princess.

Next, Jill Shalvis offers **LOVER COME BACK,** LOVESWEPT #900. As the editor of the *Heather Bay Daily News,* Justine Miller makes it her business to know what's happening in her town. But nothing could have prepared her for the shock of seeing her long-lost husband again. Not to mention the fact that he's the proud new owner of her newspaper. Two years earlier, Justine had anxiously waited for her new husband to return to their honeymoon suite. Only, Mitch Conner had disappeared, leaving Justine to deal with the embarrassment and pain. Mitch had had no choice but to leave her, but now he's back and more than eager to reclaim the love of his life. Justine refuses to believe his cockamamy story of corruption and witness protection programs. She has had her taste of marriage and love, and she's through with it. Mitch faces the toughest assignment of his life—proving to her that he'll never leave her. Jill Shalvis delivers a story of true love that can stand the test of time.

Finally, Karen Leabo brings us **THE DEVIL AND THE DEEP BLUE SEA,** LOVESWEPT #901. FBI agent Clint Nichols has a plan. Not a well-thought-out plan, but a plan nonetheless. He's going to kidnap a sister to exchange for an ex-wife. But the minute he boards the *Fortune's Smile*, Clint knows this mission will be a bust. His pretty quarry, Marissa Gabriole, pulls a gun on him and his getaway boat sinks. He's also hampered by a hurricane on the way and an accomplice who's a moron. Marissa soon grows tired of being on the run and chooses to team up with her kidnapper to flush out a mob boss. Clint isn't sure whether he can trust Marissa, but he knows it's the only way to wrap up an extensive undercover operation. Besides, what more does he have to lose? His life, for one thing. His heart, for another. Karen Leabo expertly blurs the line between what's right and what's love in this fast-paced, seaworthy caper.

Happy reading!

Susann Brailey   Joy Abella

Susann Brailey   Joy Abella

Senior Editor   Administrative Editor

P.S. Look for these women's fiction titles coming in August! Sara Donati makes her fiction debut with the hardcover publication of **INTO THE WILDERNESS,** a magnificent reading experience set in the world of *Last of the Mohicans.* Now in paperback is Glenna McReynold's **THE CHALICE AND THE BLADE,** "an enthralling, exhilarating rush of a read" (Amanda Quick) in which a runaway bride and a feared sorcerer join in a spellbinding adventure of magic and passion. In **THE LONG SHOT,** the talented and humorous Michelle Martin presents a delightful cast of characters in a story about two sisters—and one man. Susan Krinard returns with **BODY AND SOUL,** an enchanting new romance about a love so deep it will bring a man and a woman together—in another century, another life. And Leslie LaFoy follows up with **LADY RECKLESS,** as lovers fleeing across Ireland are locked in a fight for their lives and their love . . . and a fight against the Fates themselves. And immediately following this page, preview the Bantam women's fiction titles on sale in July.

For current information on Bantam's women's fiction, visit our website at the following address:
http://www.bdd.com/romance

Don't miss these extraordinary
novels from Bantam Books!

On sale in July:

WHEN VENUS FELL
by Deborah Smith

FINDING LAURA
by Kay Hooper

When Venus Fell
BY DEBORAH SMITH

*Read on for a preview of Deborah Smith's new
heartwarming novel . . .*

The stranger caught my attention like a trumpet player
blowing a high C in the middle of a harp solo.

I always drew up in a knot when a certain type of
man watched Ella and me in public. Over the years I'd
developed a knack for pinpointing the kind who considered himself the guardian of truth, justice, and the
American way. But this one stood out more than usual,
particularly in the Hers Truly. After all, he was the only
masculine patron I'd ever seen in the audience. In fact
he looked like the kind of man who'd been born with
more than an ordinary share of testosterone.

I blinked then stared again through the haze of
stage lights and cigarette smoke. *Holy freakin' moly*, as
we used to say at St. Cecilia's, when the nuns weren't
listening.

He was tall, dark and yes, bluntly handsome. But
badly worn around the edges. His face was gaunt, his
skin was pale enough to show a beard shadow even in
dim light, his mouth was appealing but too tight. He
was watching me as if I were doing a strip tease and he
was an off-duty vice cop.

Frowning, he pulled a dog-eared black-and-white
photo from his shirt pocket and held it out. For the
first time I noticed his right hand. I froze. Whoever he
was, something godawful had happened to him.

His ring finger and little finger were gone, as well
as a deep section of the knuckles at their base. His

middle finger was scarred and knotty. Lines of pink scar tissue and deep, puckered gouges snaked up his right forearm. Grotesque and awkward, the hand looked like a deformed claw.

Suddenly I was aware of my own fingers, flexing them, grateful they were all in place. He wasn't an invincible threat. He was very human, and more than a little damaged.

"Enjoying the view?" he asked tersely. I jerked my gaze to his face. Ruddy blotches of anger and embarrassment colored his cheeks. He quickly transferred the photo to his undamaged left hand and dropped the right hand into the shadows between his knees. "Have you ever seen a copy of this picture before?"

I took a deep breath and looked at the photo. A solemn, handsome young boy gazed back at me from my parents' wedding picture. There was only one copy of the picture, I thought, and I still had it. "Where did you get that?"

"It's been in my family."

"Who? What family?"

"The Camerons."

I leaned toward him, scrutinizing him helplessly. "Who *are* you?"

He pointed to the boy. "Gib Cameron," he said. "Does that mean anything to you?"

My head reeled. When I was a child I'd decided I'd never meet Gib Cameron in person but I would love him forever. That childhood memory had become a shrine to all the lost innocence in my life.

But now the shrine was real. *He* was real. "I remember your name," I said with a shrug.

"I remember yours," he said flatly. "And it's not Ann Nelson."

Gib Cameron had finally found me. It was appropriate that he knew who I really was. After all, he'd named me before I was born.

"Why are you here?" I asked warily.

He smiled with no humor. "I'm going to make you an offer you can't refuse."

MIRROR, MIRROR ON THE WALL
WHO'S THE DEADLIEST ONE OF ALL?

Finding Laura

by bestselling author

KAY HOOPER

It's an antique mirror that can reveal secrets . . . or tarnish the truth. And for struggling artist Laura Sutherland buying it is only the first step into a dark maze of lies, manipulation—and murder. It brings Peter Kilbourne into her life and makes her the prime suspect in his fatal stabbing. Determined to clear her name—and uncover Peter's reason for wanting the mirror back—Laura will breach the iron gates of the Kilbourne estate. There she will find that each family member has something to hide. Which one of them looks in the mirror and sees the reflection of the killer? And which one will choose Laura to be the next to die?

"Kay Hooper is a multitalented author whose stories
always pack a tremendous punch."
—Iris Johansen,
New York Times bestselling author

It was after five o'clock that evening when the security guard downstairs called up to tell Laura that she had a visitor.

"Who is it, Larry?"

"It's Mr. Peter Kilbourne, Miss Sutherland," the guard replied, unaware of the shock he was delivering. "He says it's in reference to the mirror you bought today."

For just an instant, Laura was conscious of nothing except an overwhelming urge to grab her mirror and run. It was nothing she could explain, but the panic was so real that Laura went ice-cold with it. Thankfully, the reaction was short-lived, since her rational mind demanded to know why on earth she felt so threatened. After all, she had bought the mirror legally, and no one had the right to take it away from her. Not even Peter Kilbourne.

Trying to shake off uneasiness, she said, "Thank you, Larry. Send him up, please."

She found her shoes and stepped into them, and absently smoothed a few strands of hair that had escaped from the long braid hanging down her back, but Laura didn't think or worry too much about how she looked. Instead, as she waited for her unexpected visitor, she stood near the couch and kept glancing at the mirror lying on several layers of newspaper on the coffee table.

It looked now, after hours of hard work, like an entirely different mirror. The rich, warm, reddish gold color of old brass gleamed now, and the elaborate pattern stamped into the metal, a shade darker, showed up vividly. It was a curious pattern, not floral as with most of the mirrors she had found, but rather a swirling series of loops and curves that were, Laura had discovered, actually made up of one continuous line—rather like a maze.

It was around the center of this maze that Laura had discovered the numbers or letters stamped into the brass, but since she hadn't yet finished polishing the back, she still didn't know what, if anything, the writing signified.

A quiet knock at her door recalled her thoughts, and Laura mentally braced herself as she went to greet her visitor. She had no particular image in her mind of

Peter Kilbourne, but she certainly didn't expect to open her door to the most handsome man she'd ever seen.

It was an actual, physical shock to see him, she realized dimly, a stab of the same astonishment one would feel if a statue of masculine perfection suddenly breathed and smiled. He was the epitome of tall, dark, and handsome—and more. Much more. Black hair, pale blue eyes, a flashing smile. Perfect features. And his charm was an almost visible thing, somehow, obvious even before he spoke in a deep, warm voice.

"Miss Sutherland? I'm Peter Kilbourne."

A voice to break hearts.

Laura gathered her wits and stepped back, opening the door wider to admit him. "Come in." She thought he was about her own age, maybe a year or two older.

He came into the apartment and into the living room, taking in his surroundings quickly but thoroughly, and clearly taking note of the mirror on the coffee table. His gaze might have widened a bit when it fell on her collection of mirrors, but Laura couldn't be sure, and when he turned to face her, he was smiling with every ounce of his charm.

It was unsettling how instantly and powerfully she was affected by that magnetism. Laura had never considered herself vulnerable to charming men, but she knew without doubt that this one would be difficult to resist—whatever it was he wanted of her. Too uneasy to sit down or invite him to, Laura merely stood with one hand on the back of a chair and eyed him with what she hoped was a faint, polite smile.

If Peter Kilbourne thought she was being ungracious in not inviting him to sit down, he didn't show it. He gestured slightly toward the coffee table and said, "I see you've been hard at work, Miss Sutherland."

She managed a shrug. "It was badly tarnished. I wanted to get a better look at the pattern."

He nodded, his gaze tracking past her briefly to once again note the collection of mirrors near the hallway. "You have quite a collection. Have you . . . always collected mirrors?"

It struck her as an odd question somehow, perhaps because there was something hesitant in his tone, something a bit surprised in his eyes. But Laura replied truthfully despite another stab of uneasiness. "Since I was a child, actually. So you can see why I bought that one today at the auction."

"Yes." He slid his hands into the pockets of his dark slacks, sweeping open his suit jacket as he did so in a pose that might have been studied or merely relaxed. "Miss Sutherland—look, do you mind if I call you Laura?"

"No, of course not."

"Thank you," he nodded gravely, a faint glint of amusement in his eyes recognizing her reluctance. "I'm Peter."

She nodded in turn, but didn't speak.

"Laura, would you be interested in selling the mirror back to me? At a profit, naturally."

"I'm sorry." She was shaking her head even before he finished speaking. "I don't want to sell the mirror."

"I'll give you a hundred for it."

Laura blinked in surprise, but again shook her head. "I'm not interested in making money, Mr. Kilbourne—"

"Peter."

A little impatiently, she said, "All right—Peter. I don't want to sell the mirror. And I did buy it legitimately."

"No one's saying you didn't, Laura," he soothed. "And you aren't to blame for my mistake, certainly.

Look, the truth is that the mirror shouldn't have been put up for auction. It's been in my family a long time, and we'd like to have it back. Five hundred."

Not a bad profit on a five-dollar purchase. She drew a breath and spoke slowly. "No. I'm sorry, I really am, but . . . I've been looking for this—for a mirror like this—for a long time. To add to my collection. I'm not interested in making money, so please don't bother to raise your offer. Even five thousand wouldn't make a difference."

His eyes were narrowed slightly, very intent on her face, and when he smiled suddenly it was with rueful certainty. "Yes, I can see that. You don't have to look so uneasy, Laura—I'm not going to wrest the thing away from you by force."

"I never thought you would," she murmured, lying.

He chuckled, a rich sound that stroked along her nerve endings like a caress. "No? I'm afraid I've made you nervous, and that was never my intention. Why don't I buy you dinner some night as an apology?"

This man is dangerous. "That isn't necessary," she said.

"I insist."

Laura looked at his incredibly handsome face, that charming smile, and drew yet another deep breath. "Will your wife be coming along?" she asked mildly.

"If she's in town, certainly." His eyes were guileless.

Very dangerous. Laura shook her head. "Thanks, but no apology is necessary. You offered a generous price for the mirror; I refused. That's all there is to it." She half turned and made a little gesture toward the door with one hand, unmistakably inviting him to leave.

Peter's beautiful mouth twisted a bit, but he obeyed the gesture and followed her to the door. When she opened it and stood back, he paused to reach into the inner pocket of his jacket and produced a business card. "Call me if you change your mind," he said. "About the mirror, I mean."

Or anything else, his smile said.

"I'll do that," she returned politely, accepting the card.

"It was nice meeting you, Laura."

"Thank you. Nice meeting you," she murmured.

He gave her a last flashing smile, lifted a hand slightly in a small salute, and left her apartment.

Laura closed the door and leaned back against it for a moment, relieved and yet still uneasy. She didn't know why Peter Kilbourne wanted the mirror back badly enough to pay hundreds of dollars for it, but every instinct told her the matter was far from settled.

She hadn't heard the last of him.

On sale in August:

INTO THE WILDERNESS
by Sara Donati

THE CHALICE AND THE BLADE
by Glenna McReynolds

BODY AND SOUL
by Susan Krinard

THE LONG SHOT
by Michelle Martin

LADY RECKLESS
by Leslie Lafoy

Jean Stone

FIRST LOVES

For every woman there is a first love, the love she never forgets. Now Meg, Zoe, and Alissa have given themselves six months to find the men who got away. But can they recover the magic they left behind? ____56343-2 $5.99/$6.99

PLACES BY THE SEA

In the bestselling tradition of Barbara Delinsky, this is the enthralling , emotionally charged tale of a woman who thought she led a charmed life...until she discovered the real meaning of friendship, betrayal, forgiveness, and love.

____57424-8 $5.99/$7.99